PIECES OF ME

PEYTON BANKS

"Love is blind despite the world's attempt to give it eyes."

Matshona Dhiwayo

CONTENTS

CHAPTER one

The pen flew across the page in smooth, easy strokes as she focused on channeling her emotions onto the crisp white paper. Nina Hunt sighed as she relaxed into the plush recliner in her study, staring out the window at the beautiful gardens that lined her yard, waiting for the next word to come to her.

Writing was a way for her to work through her emotions. She had built her career from writing some of the most popular songs to ever grace the music industry.

She was Nina Hunt—singer, songwriter, megastar.

She had been described as one of the most successful black musicians of all-time. Having accomplished so much in her career, she looked around and saw everything that she had earned by the pen in her hand touching paper.

It was because of a dare from her sister to enter that fateful talent contest. After winning, Lewis "Key" Edwards offered her a deal with Steel City Entertainment, and within a year, she had recorded her first album at the young age of seventeen.

Her parents had pushed for her to go to college, stressing to her that music could not be a guarantee, and they wanted her to have a backup plan. They came up with an agreement—one album, and if it didn't do well, she would enroll into college.

Her first album released when she was nineteen years old, and she became a household name. Her debut album, titled A Foolish Gamble, rendered her four top singles on the Billboard Hot 100 and earned her four Grammys.

Even though the deal with her parents had paid off, she still went to college, thanks to online studies, earning herself a degree in business that she had been able to use throughout her career in the music industry.

She glanced around her plush study, which was her special getaway in her house. This room was where she felt safe and secure, and could let her creative juices flow.

She was finally off her major world tour and could do as she pleased, and what she wanted to do was write. Most of her songs were based off her or a friend's life experiences. But lately, her writings had turned to channel her broken heart. The only way that she would be able to heal from her very public breakup with her ex-boyfriend was to write.

Being in the spotlight never gave her the chance to experience anything in private, so she chose to plan an album where she could document her private thoughts.

"Thank goodness for publicists," she grumbled to herself as she pushed her dark hair from her eyes. Rose Wall, her faithful publicist, had her hands full right now. As Nina relaxed in her home and tried to get acclimated to being back in the States, her poor publicist had been trying to handle the media.

The media had been in a frenzy since the news leaked that action movie star Luke Stow and R&B sensation Nina Hunt were no longer a couple. He had certainly done a number on her. Her eyes clouded over as the memories began to appear.

"This isn't going to work between us anymore," Luke informed her, his dark eyes cold as he stared at her. Tears streamed down her face as she stared at the man who she had been in what she thought was a loving relationship. She knew neither of them had been ready for marriage, but she'd thought that eventually, they would.

Both of them were at the top of their respected careers. Luke was one of the most sought-after action hero. His smooth chocolate complexion had graced the covers of magazines and at least a dozen films, but now as she stared into his eyes, it was as if she were looking at a stranger.

"Why are you doing this?" she cried out, running a

shaky hand through her hair. She turned away from him and walked over to the window of her luxury hotel room to stare out at the magical lights of the Louvre, afraid she would say or do something crazy as her heart shattered. She angrily wiped the tears.

Paris, the City of Lights.

Tonight was supposed to be a night of celebration. It was the last stop on her world tour, and instead of having a great time with friends and her band, he was there in her hotel room to put an end to their three-year relationship.

"You've changed," he admitted. She turned sharply, brushing the tears from her face.

"What are you talking about?" she demanded to know. She refused to believe that he could stand there and tell her that she was no longer the same person he'd first met.

"Well, you know..." He fumbled with his words as he waved his hands at her body.

"No, I don't know. Why don't you tell me," she demanded, anger rising in her chest. She refused to put words in his mouth, wanting to hear exactly how she had changed. Her eyes narrowed on him as his eyes trailed down her body.

The bastard.

"You've put on some pounds lately," he began, suddenly looking away from her.

"You have got to be fucking kidding me!" she snapped,

4

stalking toward him. She stopped in front of him and waited for a response.

For all the years they had known each other, he knew she had struggled with her weight. They had met ten years ago on the set of a movie, and had been friends for years before becoming a power couple.

The media also loved to point out her struggles with her weight. She was never a size two or four as the media and fashion designers had always demanded.

Sure, she was thick, but this was the best she'd felt in a long time. On tour, the amount of dancing and singing always ensured that her weight was maintained. The chefs and cooks that toured with her made sure that her diet was healthy to help give her the strength and support her body needed while under the stresses of touring.

"Screaming doesn't fix anything, Nina. I just can't do this anymore." He shook his head and turned to walk away, but she grabbed his arm and forced him to turn to her.

"So that's it?"

Damn, the tears. She didn't want to appear weak in front of him, but dammit, she really did care for him—she loved him.

Luke looked at her, regret reflecting in his eyes. He pulled his arm away from her and backed up.

"Yeah, that's it." He turned and walked out of her hotel room and out of her life.

She stood there, shocked and confused as the tears continued to flow down her cheeks.

"Oh boy! You're in your writing chair." A familiar voice interrupted her trip down memory lane.

She turned and found her sister leaning against the doorframe, with a small smile on her lips. Nina didn't have to look closer at her sister to see the pity in her eyes. She knew her expressions well. Meg's smooth, caramel skin practically glowed against the white summer dress that flowed around her.

"Well, writing is how I make money. The tour may be over, but my writing never stops," she said, a wistful smile on her lips.

"Nina, you've been moping around in this big ass house of yours for the last few weeks since we got home from Paris. You can't stay in here like a hermit," Meg nagged as she marched into the room with a determined look on her face.

"I can do as I damn well please. I have literally been on the road for six months. What's the use of having a home if I'm not going to enjoy it?" Nina rolled her eyes. It was good to be home. She wasn't quite ready to go out in public yet and have to deal with the media.

That was the major downfall to life as a famous musician. It was rare she could go out and not be recognized. Paparazzi followed her everywhere, leading her to hire a full-time security team.

"Luke was an asshat, and so not worth you getting depressed. We need to get you out of this house and show the world that Nina Hunt doesn't need a man," Meg said, kneeling down next to her. Her eyes were wide as she pleaded with Nina, the younger of the two siblings.

"I'm okay, Meg. I've thought about our relationship and now my blinders are off. I didn't want to believe it, but there were problems."

"I can't believe he brought up your weight. I didn't think he was that shallow. You're beautiful, and the whole world thinks so. Why can't he?"

Nina had asked herself that at least a thousand times. She may have gained about twenty pounds, but she actually liked her curves. She felt empowered, and even felt sexy. Some women paid big money to add the extra cushion in the spots that she carried hers. She'd seen articles in magazines about her ass, and there was even a page on social media dedicated to it.

Nina knew that Meg was right. She didn't need a man, but they sure were nice to have around for certain activities. She laughed internally, thinking of her and Luke's sex life. It had been good—not life-changing, but she had been happy with it.

She never complained. She knew her sister would not give up until she felt that Nina was healing.

But Nina knew what would help her.

Writing.

She'd been home the last few weeks and had penned eight full songs already. This was how she healed. This was her therapy.

"I'm okay, Meg. Seriously, I am. I've even had the big cry already. No more tears. Luke can move on for all I care."

Her heart wasn't as heavy as the first night after Luke walked out on her. She knew that her world would not end because Luke Stow was no longer with her. But she spoke the truth. She refused to cry any more tears over Luke Stow.

She had a plan.

"Uh-oh, I know that look," Meg groaned, shaking her head. She stood up and walked over to the chaise against the wall, plopping down onto it. "Go ahead, tell me the plan."

Shit. Her sister could read her too well, and she would have to. Not only was she the elder sibling, but she worked as Nina's personal assistant. Nina wouldn't trust anyone else but her sister.

"Right now, all I will say is that I need you to get in touch with Scott."

"You're ready to get back in the studio already? I thought you had strict orders from your manager, Tasha, to take the next few months off and just live. Enjoy yourself, go on vacation, and enjoy the money you just earned from this tour."

Her six-month tour had brought in over two hundred million dollars, being one of the largest tours she'd been on with thirty cities in the States and eighteen in Europe. She knew that she should at least treat herself, but at the moment, there was nothing better than being home.

"This is personal, having nothing to do with the label or management. This is for me."

"Calling in Scott is an expensive therapy," Meg grumbled, leaning back.

Scott Rich was a major powerhouse producer and a dear friend of Nina's. Whenever the two of them got together in the studio, magic happened. He was very expensive, but with the money Nina had pulled in over the years, she could easily afford him without batting an eye.

"Get him," she replied. She had ideas filling her head. Her heart began to pound as she thought of getting into the studio with Scott. "We're going to use the studio here."

She glanced down at her notebook and felt a weight being lifted from her shoulders. She'd be the first to admit that Luke hurt her and broke her heart, and it would take some time to get over him.

"Okay, I'll call him. But first, we're going out to

lunch," Meg announced. Walking over to Nina, she pulled her from the chair.

"Meg!" Nina cried out, laughing as she tried to hold onto her notebook. "You're crazy."

"You pay me a lot of money to assist you and I'm going to do my job. Starting with putting your ass in the shower!"

"I don't stink!" Nina laughed, trying to get a whiff of her underarm as her sister dragged her through her mansion.

"I smelled you from the doorway when I first arrived."

"Bitch!"

"You love this bitch," Meg retorted.

Nina smiled as her sister pushed her into her bedroom. She placed her notebook on the nightstand by her bed before turning to Meg.

"I love you, sis," she said, feeling a tingling at the back of her throat. *I will not cry. I will not cry.* What would she do without her sister? She hoped to never find out.

"I love you too. Now go!" Meg pointed to the en suite bathroom. "I'll pick you out something sexy to wear while you shower."

"Okay," Nina grumbled as she stomped her feet like a small child. She loved her close relationship with her sister and couldn't have asked for a better sibling. Nina stepped over to the shower and quickly stripped off her clothes. She started the shower and waited for the warm temperature to regulate.

She was strong and would get over Luke Stow. Today, her sister must have known that she needed a swift kick in the ass. It was time for her show her face in public. She would move forward and live her life.

CHAPTER
two

Today there will be a VIP client stopping by the gym to meet with you for a consultation.

Sid reread the text again on his cell phone.

VIP client? he thought to himself.

He dialed his longtime friend and owner of Unlimited Fitness, Kevin Decker. When Kevin had approached him with the notion of the gym, Sid jumped right in. Kevin appointed Sid as the general manager and lead personal trainer. Unlimited Fitness was a trendy luxury health club that catered to all clients.

"Yo, Sid! You get my text?" Kevin greeted him, a little too happily for it being six in the morning. Sid had yet to grab his coffee yet. Once he'd had about two cups or so, he usually started to be personable.

"What do you mean, VIP client?" Sid asked as he approached the building. He hoisted his duffle bag on his shoulder as he walked through the automatic doors.

"This could mean big business if this client decides to use our facility and services."

Sid waved to a few employees as he made his way through the club toward his office. What client here in Cleveland would draw business to the club?

"Who is it?" Sid asked, pulling his key from his sweatpants. He unlocked his office door and flipped the light on as he walked into the small room. It wasn't much, but it was his office. Kevin paid him a damn good salary to manage the facility. They were in the planning phase of opening another one, and if Kevin thought taking on a VIP client would help, then Sid was all ears.

"Nina Hunt," Kevin announced.

The name sounded familiar, but he couldn't put a face to it. He thought hard as he tossed his keys on the desk and dropped his bag onto the windowsill behind his desk. Plopping down in his chair, he turned his computer on.

"Nina Hunt?"

"You have got to be shitting me! You don't know who Nina Hunt is?" Kevin's incredulous voice came through the phone.

"Am I supposed to?"

"What stone do you live under?" Kevin muttered under his breath. "Look, she'll be there soon. Maybe it's best you don't know her. She wanted to come before the club opens so no other clients would be there. Show her around and answer her questions."

"Why is she coming here?" Sid asked, logging into the club's system.

"Because she wants to get in shape. She had a very public breakup and it's been all over the media. According to the Hot List, her boyfriend broke up with her because she'd gained too much weight."

What an ass, Sid thought, shaking his head. What man wanted a woman who was skin and bones? Sid had always been a man who loved his women to have some cushion. He was a big man and didn't want to feel as if he would break his woman in half.

"All right." Sid sighed as he leaned back in his chair. "I'll win her over with my charm and have her sign on as a client."

He didn't really have time to play trainer with a celebrity, but if Kevin thought it would help the club, he'd do it. He'd rather help those who were really in need of guidance to a healthier lifestyle because there was nothing more satisfying then helping someone change their lives for the better. He'd show the superstar the gym, probably only see her a few times so she could get her photos for the media to show that she was working out, and then he'd probably never see her again.

"Just please, make sure she signs on. I'll be there after I take my mom to her doctor's appointment."

"Everything okay?" Sid asked, running his hand through his still damp hair from his early morning shower.

"Yeah, she just has her yearly physical. Her eyesight is getting worse and she just wanted me to drive her," Kevin informed him.

"See you when you get here." Sid disconnected the call, just as the phone on his desk rang.

"Hello?" Sid greeted.

"Hey, Sid." Ivy's excited voice came through the line. It was just way too early for everyone to be this damn excited. Sid yawned, as he could practically hear Ivy bouncing in her chair through the connection.

"What's up, Ivy?" Another yawn claimed him.

"You'll never believe who's here," she whispered.

He chuckled at the excitement that lined her voice. "Who is it, Ivy?"

"Nina. Fucking. Hunt!" she practically screamed. He pulled the phone away from his ear to save his eardrum.

"I hope you're being professional, Ivy." He rolled his eyes at the sounds of her giggles. This lady would probably think Ivy was crazy and leave before he could even rescue her from their overzealous receptionist.

"Yes, I am. She said she had an appointment with you."

"I'm on my way." He hung up the phone without waiting for a reply.

Curiosity was getting the best of him, but he didn't have time to look her up now. He got up and walked out of his office to make his way to the front lobby. He realized that he didn't even ask Kevin why she was a celebrity. He prayed that it was not because of reality television. He couldn't stand reality television, preferring scripted shows where people with real talent could entertain him.

Sid made his way to their lounge. Kevin had wanted Unlimited Fitness to have a resort feel, wanting every person who came through their doors to change their life to feel special. The lounge was where their clients waited to meet with their potential trainers. It was decked out with plush furniture and televisions to keep the clients entertained while they waited.

He entered the room and was first met with the cool eyes of a mammoth of a man in dark clothes, standing in the middle of the room. The guy stood at least three inches taller than Sid's six foot three. His dark eyes landed on Sid.

"Mrs. Hunt?" he called out, looking around the room.

"I'm here," a husky voice announced from behind the mammoth. "Tank, move." Her chuckle caused his cock to twitch. He realized fast that he would love to hear it again.

Tank? Yeah, that name fit the guy perfectly. Sid's eyes landed on the female who walked from around Tank, and his breath caught in his throat as he took in the smooth bronze complexion of her skin. Her face was free of makeup and stunningly perfect. Her dark hair flowed around her shoulders and gently rested on her generous mounds. He quickly recovered as he realized she was waiting on him.

"Hi, Mrs.—"

"It's Miss," she corrected him. Her hazel eyes held a curious look to them as he held his hand out to her. Her white summer dress flowed around her legs as she leaned forward to take his hand.

"I'm Sid," he greeted as they shared a strong handshake. Her small hand was engulfed by his larger one, and a warm sensation zipped up his arm at her touch. He found himself not wanting to let it go.

"Please, call me Nina," she murmured, pulling her hand back, and he instantly missed the warmth. "I spoke to Kevin Decker, and he told me that you were the best in the city."

"Well, it depends on what services you need," he replied, then coughed, realizing what he'd said. She only smiled, revealing perfect white teeth. He watched as she tucked her dark hair behind her small brown ear, revealing three diamond earrings in her lobe.

"Well, I'm looking forward to getting into shape."

"Let me give you a tour of the club, then we can sit down and discuss exactly what you're looking for. I'm sure I can help fulfill your needs."

Fuck.

He did it again. He didn't know what the hell his problem was. Who was talking? His brain or his cock?

She chuckled again and nodded her head. "That sounds good."

His cock twitched again, and he tried to think of anything that would calm it down.

He walked back over to the door from which he came and held it open for her and Tank. "Welcome to Unlimited Fitness."

Nina knew that Sid was talking, but she didn't hear a word he'd said. Her eyes were drawn to his strong chest and thick, muscular arms. Even through his T-shirt, she could see the outline of his muscles. Her fingers itched to touch him. She didn't know why, but she wanted to try to wrap her hands around his biceps. Her small hands wouldn't fit, but she wanted to feel what his hard muscles would feel like underneath her fingers.

His clear blue eyes captivated her the moment she'd walked around Tank. The way his eyes moved along her body left her feeling as if he was caressing it with his hands. Her nipples beaded tight as his eyes paused at her full breasts. She had her times when she was shy and insecure with all of her flaws, but right now, she didn't feel any of them. She felt like a woman by the time Sid was finished looking her over.

Luke had certainly been one to bring out her flaws, like how she was overweight. But she didn't see any complaints in Sid's eyes.

She felt comfortable in her own skin. But now, she would show Luke and the world that she could get healthier. She didn't want to lose all of her curves, but she had a few areas that could be tightened and toned. She wanted to accent her best features, and felt that it was best she seek professional help. Her and Meg searched for the best fitness club in their hometown of Cleveland, Ohio.

Unlimited Fitness came up in their search and Meg had called to look into the club. According to the owner, they would be able to meet her demands of a private trainer. Sid McFarland came highly recommended.

"We have state of the art equipment if you want to jump on a treadmill, a stair climber, or an elliptical." Sid pointed where rows of the machines were kept, along with weight training areas that were placed in front of mirrors.

She looked around the room and imagined how many people would be in the room. It turned her off. Not that she minded working out around people, but she knew that most of them wouldn't be working out. They would be too busy trying to film her on their phones. Maybe this wasn't the best idea.

"How many people come here daily?" Tank asked. He must have seen the look on her face and read her mind. That's why Tank was her bodyguard, and a good friend too. He had worked for her for years, and was very protective of her.

"Well, I don't know the numbers daily, but this is a popular place for people to come work out. From what Kevin told me when I spoke to him briefly this morning, you wanted privacy, and here, we can accommodate you."

"How?" she asked, turning back to him. Her heart sped up at the intensity of his gaze.

"Follow me." His lips turned up in the corner before he turned, motioning for her to follow him. She couldn't take her eyes off of him.

I'd follow him anywhere, she thought with a chuckle. Her eyes dropped down to his ass and she sighed.

Tank's thick forearm gently pushed her, causing her

to stumble slightly. She glanced up at him quickly and he shook his head.

He had caught her, and she smiled as she stuck her tongue out at him, causing him to roll his eyes.

She was single and could look. Nothing was wrong with looking. She was here to get herself healthy, and if Sid was going to be her trainer, then she would at least have some nice eye candy.

"Here we are. This private gym was just recently added on for private clients such as yourself." Sid turned as he opened the door to another room. This one was an enclosed room that offered a few machines, weights, and even a mat for aerobics. It was a mini version of the general area.

She walked into the room and slowly made her way around. She was pleased. It would provide her with everything she would need.

"This will be perfect." She smiled as she walked up to Sid, whose eyes had yet to look away from her. She liked it. Again, she felt like a woman. She could feel her core clench as his eyes dropped to her lips. "So what would you recommend for someone like me who just wants to tone a few places and not lose my curves?"

CHAPTER
three

A good fucking.

By him.

That's what exercise regime he would recommend for her. Sweaty, body jarring, headboard banging, heart pounding sex—the best workout. He'd fuck her until neither of them could move. Everyone knew that sex burned calories. He just needed to lock them in a bedroom for two weeks and they'd both lose weight.

He was attracted to her.

Just a little.

Who the hell was he kidding? If he could, he'd strip them both down now and take her; slide his thick length into her tight little pussy.

Fuck.

Kevin said to get her to commit to using their facility, not drool over her. Hell, just thinking of helping her stretch her muscles out had him stiff as a board.

"Well, what areas are you trying to target?" he asked,

trying to stay professional. Plus, the daggers that her mountain of a bodyguard was shooting him let him know the guard knew what he was thinking. He made a mental note to never meet him in a dark alley.

"Well..." She looked down at herself, and he couldn't help but look too.

She's perfect the way she is, he thought to himself.

"I would like to tighten up my tummy, my hips, and my ass," she announced, looking at him.

Her ass. He held back a groan. He had already checked it out, and it was a delicious ass. One he would love to sink his teeth into.

"Okay, we can definitely design a plan for you. Anything else?" he asked, trying to stay focused. He had done consultations a million times, but never with anyone who he wanted to go full barbarian on. He wanted to snatch her up and throw her over his shoulder, claiming her.

"Honestly, I just want to work on becoming healthier overall. I don't want to be skinny, I want to be curvy. No hard muscles. I want to stay soft and feminine. Does that make sense?" she asked with a tilt of her head.

He jerked his head in a nod. "Yeah, I got you. Let's go to my office where we can discuss diet plans, and I can draw up your invoice."

"Money isn't a problem, Sid."

He looked sharply at her as she walked alongside

him. He guided them toward his office and again, he wished he would have taken the few seconds to look her up.

"Okay, cool."

He ushered her into the small office. Tank decided to wait on the outside, as if wanting to keep anyone from rushing in. He waved her to a seat as he rounded his desk.

"You have no idea who I am, do you?" she asked, crossing her legs. His eyes were drawn to the smooth brown skin of her calves.

"Not a clue," he admitted. She smiled that perfect smile that got his heart thumping away.

"Good." She nodded and relaxed back in the chair.

He began to ask her questions about her diet, and offered opinions on how she could improve on it. He mentioned seeing the dietician that they employed at the health center to help her learn better food choices.

He tried his best to stay focused, but every time she laughed, his cock stood at attention.

"So, for what you're requesting, here's the first month's invoice. Look it over and let me know if it's okay." He grabbed a sheet of paper from his printer. It would be a little pricey, more than what they charged regular patrons of the club. Since she was requiring everything private, it was more. Kevin had been looking into branching out, offering full-time private trainer services for exclusive clients for a while now, but the opportunity had not presented itself until now.

"It's fine," she said, without even looking at it. Her hazel eyes twinkled, as if she were holding back a laugh. "My business manager will take care of it, and will pay the entire year."

He tried not to act surprised. She did say that money was not an issue.

"Okay, great. Now, with this new model that we're offering, it comes along with perks. Training doesn't have to be all here. We can meet at parks, your house, or wherever you would want to work out. So between you and I, we can work out exactly where we'll train, then I can design a workout based along that."

"That sounds great. Sometimes, it's hard for me to go out in public, so being able to have you come to my house or parks is nice. I have a large property, and it's beautiful in the summertime."

"Good." He smiled at her. The conversation died out, but it wasn't uncomfortable. Their eyes connected as they both took each other in.

"So, when do we begin?" she asked, her voice breaking into his very inappropriate thoughts. Visions of her naked brown skin against his tan skin came to mind, causing him to become unbearably hard.

"Um, tomorrow?" he asked. He could barely think.

All the blood in his body had rushed south. She smiled and stood with her hand outstretched.

"I expect you to stay on me," she said as he stood to take her hand.

"Huh?" Yeah, no blood flow to the brain. He blinked a few times while looking at her. *Stay on her?* He could definitely oblige that request.

"You know, make sure I don't stray away from the plan."

"Yes, of course." He smiled sheepishly as he let her hand go.

Right.

Not literally on her.

That wouldn't be professional.

"It was nice to meet you, Sid." She smiled as she walked toward the door, and he quickly rushed around his desk to open it for her. Surprise crossed her face as his hand grasped the door handle first.

"It was a pleasure to meet you too, Nina," he said softly. Her eyes darkened at she looked up at him. He loved how he towered over her. A protective nature came over him as he turned the handle and opened the door.

"Such a gentleman," she murmured, her lips turning up in a small smile. She walked through the door, her hips swaying as she walked away. He glanced up and caught Tank's narrowed eyes.

Busted.

He rolled his eyes as they walked away. What man wouldn't look at an ass as plump as hers?

***

"I don't like him," Tank announced as he pulled the car out of the parking lot.

Nina settled back into the plush, luxury sedan. The sun was certainly out today. She reached down and grabbed her sunglasses out of her handbag. Hiding behind her shades, she looked up and found Tank looking at her through the rearview mirror.

"And why not? He seems nice," she exclaimed. She hit the button on the side of the door that would raise the leg rest up. She loved this car. It was one of the most luxurious cars that money could buy, and was well worth it. She could relax while being driven around.

"He couldn't keep his eyes off of you. That was unprofessional if you ask me. You're coming to him for help, and he was basically drooling over you like he wanted to gobble you up."

Nina barked out a laugh at Tank's description. He glared at her through the mirror.

"I just think he was being very focused on my weaknesses, and I'm sure he was thinking of designing me a workout plan for all the places on me that I complained about." She shook her head and stared out the tinted windows at the scenery as it passed by. Tank could be a little overprotective. They had worked together for so long, she looked to him as a brother, and she knew that the feelings were mutual.

"I'm a man, and I know all about those looks he was giving you. He was definitely looking at you as a man who sees a woman he wants."

"Is that so bad? It was actually nice to have someone look at me like a woman," she scoffed. Most people looked at her as a superstar, a paycheck, a moneymaker. Or better yet, a singer who was overweight. It was actually nice to feel the heat of a man's stare. Her core still pulsed with the thought of his blue eyes looking up at her as he tasted her.

"Did you forget one little thing?" Tank asked with an eyebrow raised.

"What? He doesn't know who I am. Well, I'm sure he will now once he googles me. But he wasn't acting. He didn't have a clue as to who I am," she said, brushing her hair out her face.

"Not that. You did look at him, right?"

"Of course I did. We just spent an hour with him." She tilted her head to the side, trying to think of what Tank could be talking about.

"He's a white guy, Nina, and you're black."

Nina stared at Tank, as if he sprouted horns on his

head. She couldn't even believe this was coming out of his mouth.

"Tank, are you racist?"

"What? Hell no. I'm just stating the obvious."

"So a white guy can't desire a black woman?" she asked. This was the twenty-first century!

"I'm not saying that. But the media will be in a frenzy over this." Tank shook his head as he turned the car down the road leading to her private estate.

"Well, you're acting like I've already fucked the guy and I'm ready to marry him. All I said was that I liked the way he looked at me," she snapped, turning back to the scenery.

"Don't go getting mad at me. You know I'm always honest. Hell, you know I'll take a bullet for you any day, but I don't want you getting hurt again."

She huffed, mulling over his words. She sighed, knowing he was right. No matter what year it was, some people would have a problem with any little thing, even a mixed raced couple. Well, it was none of society's business who she chose to sleep with or not.

If she wanted to pour a little cream in her coffee, that was her choice.

"What do you have planned today?" Tank asked.

"Scott should be arriving today. I had an idea and he's going to help me."

"Sweet. I haven't seen Scott since the Grammy

awards last year." She was thankful that he changed the subject. Race relations was a little too deep of a conversation this early in the morning. She was thankful that Sid was able to see her at six in the morning, before their club opened so she could avoid a crowd.

"Yeah, he didn't come to this year's awards show because he was doing a few shows across Europe."

She opened up the console that divided the two seats and pulled her iPad out as an idea sprang into her head. She loved how her ideas came out of nowhere sometimes. Because of that, she kept certain devices everywhere that could link up together to share her files across all of them. She grabbed her pointer and began to write.

She thought of the feelings that had rumbled in her abdomen just thinking of Sid. The lyrics flowed from her heart and onto the tablet. What better way to speak to the world than by a song? She had millions of followers and fans, and writing was a way for her to express herself. She wasn't always the best at verbalizing her feelings, but if a person read her lyrics or listened to her albums, they would know she poured her heart and soul into her work.

It didn't matter what she sung about. Once she stepped up to the microphone, the world would become her captive audience.

CHAPTER
four

Sid stepped from his bathroom, tired from the long day's work. He tucked his towel around his waist as he made his way to his king-sized bed. Dropping down, he grabbed his phone from his nightstand. The club was in a buzz about having Nina there. The employees were not allowed to discuss her being in the club, but it didn't stop them from speaking amongst each other.

He'd been so busy with his clients and managerial duties that he never got the time to Google her. Apparently, she was some world-renowned singer. Ivy and the other girls were fighting over who would get her water and whatever else she needed. He'd pretty much ignored them, lost in his own fantasies that were a little more X-rated.

He pulled up the internet on his smart phone, typed in her name, and watched as an endless amount of results came up. To the right of his screen, her sultry picture stared back at him. His breath was ripped from his lungs as he looked at her creamy bronze skin. Her long dark hair flowed around her shoulders, and her eyes were smoky and sexy, thanks to an expert makeup artist. Her lips were full, plump, and painted a bright red. He couldn't help but imagine those lips wrapped around his cock.

The playful twinkle in her eyes brought a smile to his face. His eyes dropped down to her net worth and he almost dropped his phone.

"Shit," he breathed.

Four hundred million dollars.

His eyes flew down her discography and saw that she had hit after hit over the years. Some songs he recognized from movie soundtracks, others from television commercials or the radio. He wasn't really into R&B music. From time to time, he did find a song or two that made their way into his playlist, but he never knew who any of the singers were. He just knew good music when he heard it.

Now that he looked at her picture again, he did remember her performing at the halftime show of the Super Bowl game a couple of years ago.

"Wow," he breathed, but it wasn't her money that impressed him. It was the person he had actually met. For someone who had the superstar status that she had, she was truly down-to-earth. He remembered the pleased look that she had on her face when she realized that he didn't know who she was. That let him know that fame and fortune hadn't gone to her head. She was just a regular girl who was trying to get into shape.

And he wanted to fuck her.

More than just fuck her—he wanted to possess her.

His cock hardened just looking at her picture on the internet. He began scrolling through some of her more provocative photos, unable to look away. He hadn't even realized he had moved the towel from his groin area until the chilled air brushed along the length of his hardened member.

His eyes were locked on a picture of her in a barely-there outfit. Her brown legs were displayed fully. Her shorts were so short, the bottom meat of her ass hung out. She was bent over the back of a chaise, poised to allow the cameraman to shoot her picture.

Her facial expression caused lust to slam into his chest. It was as if she were looking directly at him, wanting him. His hand slid down to his cock and encircled the tip. He grunted as the feel of his rough callouses connected with the sensitive tip of his dick.

He imagined Nina there with him, guiding her hand along his thickness. Her small hands would slide with his to guide the head between those plump brown lips of hers. She didn't need the makeup they had on her in the picture.

She was a knockout without it.

She'd take him deep into the back of her throat, her

tongue caressing him as if to welcome him. He began to pump his hand as he continued his little fantasy. He could hear her moans of pleasure in his head, causing him to thrust into his hand, imagining her swallowing him as far as she could.

He stared at her hazel eyes in the photograph, imaging them staring up at him as she kneeled on the floor before him. He ached to run his fingers through her hair to guide her along. He leaned back on his bed and closed his eyes as he continued to think of fucking her perfect little mouth.

His thoughts changed from her on her knees in front of him, to him behind her, slamming his cock deep within her slick core. Her plump ass would shake from the force of his thrusts. It didn't take long for him to bring himself to completion with his fantasy. That familiar tingling sensation from deep within his balls appeared as he pictured his cock disappearing within her folds.

He grunted as his release burst forth, spewing into his cupped hand. His breaths came fast as he tried to get himself under control, pumping a couple more times to finish milking his release. His hand paused as a thought came to mind.

He needed her.

But he knew that he wouldn't be able to have her. She was way out of his league.

Nina tried to hold back her yawn as she walked into Unlimited Fitness, but failed. She had been in the studio half the night before turning into bed. Her good friend Scott was in town, and their studio session was just like old times.

Today, she decided to drive herself. She drove one of her dark luxury sedans, put a baseball cap on her head, and oversized sunglasses to hide her identity. It had actually felt good to go out in public alone.

She walked through the private entrance of the club that Sid had showed her. Through this entrance, no one would see her come and go except other VIP patrons.

She was prepared to work out today. She wore mesh, black cropped leggings with a matching sports bra, and a hot pink jacket to cover her up until she was ready to start her work out. Comfortable shoes completed her outfit. She hoisted her bag up higher on her shoulder as she made her way to the private workout area.

"Few minutes early on the first day." Sid's voice appeared behind her. Her heart did a little pitter-patter at the sound of his voice.

"Yeah, I'm a little excited." She smiled as he walked closer to her.

She was thankful for her sunglasses as she took all of him in. Dark knee-length performance shorts and matching compression tank highlighted his drool worthy body.

She swallowed hard at the bare muscles in his arms as he waved her into the private workout area. She placed her belongings in the locker that was assigned for her and quickly removed her jacket, throwing it in there too before slamming the door shut. She turned and found Sid's eyes greedily taking her in.

Nerves set in as she thought of what was to come. It had been a long while since she had actually worked out. On tour, she would participate in the dancing routines, but she wouldn't go full-out dancing like her dancers, due to the simple fact she had to sing.

"I thought we would start with some strength training, but first, let's go ahead and stretch. We want to do this to loosen up your muscles."

She nodded as she joined him over at the mat. He guided her in deep stretches to get her to loosen up, but she would have sworn it was doing the opposite. Her body was strung tight watching him demonstrate, doing the same moves next to her. She tried her best to push every erotic thought that came to her out of her mind. She was here to get herself healthy.

Not laid.

She lost track of time as they continued. Her body worked up quite a sweat as he put her through the circuits he'd designed for her. She had thought that they would just do the treadmill or the elliptical.

Boy, was she wrong.

He had her working on every part of her body. She had a feeling she was going to be sore tomorrow.

"You're doing good. Do twelve more reps," he encouraged, his blue eyes locked on her as she did her squats.

She grunted as she dipped low, watching herself in the mirror. Her face was drenched in sweat and her muscles burned a hot heat with each movement.

"I don't think I can do twelve," she gasped as she came back up. Her legs trembled with the deep movement.

"Yes, you can. Push through it. Dig deep," he urged. Coming to stand beside her, he began doing them with her.

She glanced over at him and dug deep down inside of herself. She could do this.

"Eight. Nine. Ten." He counted and she closed her eyes tight, letting his deep, baritone voice roll over her. Just the sound of his voice turned her on. She tried to change the train of her thoughts because now was not the time to get all worked up. "Eleven. Twelve."

"Holy moly!" she exclaimed as she stood erect, hands on her hips. Her breaths were coming hard and fast as sweat dripped down her face and slid down between her breasts. Her clothes were drenched, and she knew she looked like a hot mess. She tried to take a few steps, but her legs were jelly. She flopped down on the mat and laughed.

"Way to push through it," he chuckled as he came and sat down next to her.

"I'm so going to pay for this tomorrow, aren't I?" she asked between breaths. At this point, she didn't care what she looked like.

"Probably, but we're going to push through it tomorrow too."

"Tomorrow? Hell, I don't foresee me getting up from this mat. Just leave me be, I'll probably just waste away here. After the funeral, just make sure my headstone says 'killed by her workout,'" she giggled.

He chuckled as he looked at her. Her breath caught in her throat as he gently reached over and brushed her hair away from her forehead. Her heart pounded as she imagined more, but she bit her lip.

"You'll live another day." His eyes darkened as they dropped down to her lips. She couldn't help but stare at his. They looked soft, and she wondered what they would feel like on hers. "We should go get in the jacuzzi," he murmured.

"We?" she asked. Her core clenched with the thought of him in the jacuzzi tub with her.

"I mean you," he grunted, pulling back from her

and getting to his feet. He turned and offered his hand to her. Disappointment filled her with the thought of not being able to see his chest without his shirt.

She grasped his hand and he easily pulled her to her feet. She stumbled as she stood, her body colliding with his. His hand automatically gripped her hip to steady her.

She knew it was a dirty move, but she was dying to feel his body against hers, and if this was the only way, so be it.

"I'm sorry," she whispered as she stared up into his eyes, before dropping down to his lips. She pressed closer to him.

"Nina." Her name was torn from his chest in a growl, right before his mouth crashed onto hers. She parted her lips to grant him entrance. His tongue pushed forward, sweeping her mouth, tasting her. She reached up on her tiptoes to get closer to him, sliding her hands up to his hair. His lips were just as soft as she imagined they would be.

A moan escaped from her as his hand slid to her bottom, pulling her closer to him, his bulge pushing against her stomach. He broke the kiss and started trailing his lips down her jaw.

"Sid," she moaned his name, loving the feel of his tongue swirling against her neck. His body stiffened for a moment before relaxing as he rested his forehead against hers.

"We can't do this." His voice was filled with regret.

"Why not?" she asked, her heart pounding. She was ready to strip her clothes off her body and throw him to the ground.

"Because this isn't right," he said with a shake of his head. He released her and took a couple steps away, turning his back to her. She stared at it, still trying to catch her breath.

"What isn't right?" she asked, pushing the hair that had fallen from her ponytail behind her ear. Her heart sank as she thought about Tank's words. She desperately needed to know what wouldn't work. "Is it because I'm black?"

"What?" He flew around with wide eyes and stalked back to her. When he stopped, she tilted back her head so that she could look up into his eyes. "I think you're the most beautiful woman I have ever met. Even now, after your workout, I want you."

"Then what are you saying?" she asked as he reached up to cup her face. She felt some relief that it wasn't a skin color thing. She knew that everyone wasn't as how Tank put it. His thumb gently caressed her bottom lip, swollen from his kiss. She unconsciously leaned against his hand, loving how their skin looked together.

"Because of who you are and who I am," he admitted, pulling his hand away.

"So you googled me?"

"Yeah, and from what I know, you're totally out of my league." He ran a shaky hand through his hair and stepped away from her, again. It hurt to have him move away from her.

"I don't get a say in this?" she huffed in disbelief, standing with her fists firm on her hips. What the hell? What was wrong with getting to know each other and fooling around?

"From now on, let's keep it platonic, Nina. I should have never touched you."

CHAPTER
five

"Today, I only want me, Scott, and Bill in the studio," Nina informed Meg as they made their way down to her in-house studio. That was one of the perks of being one of the biggest superstars; she didn't have to pay for studio time. She built her own right on her property.

The studio was housed in a building that she had built on the other side of her estate. It had a walkway that led from the main house, and even had a driveway for when guests came to use it. When she was in town, she would open her studio up to starving musicians who didn't have the money to pay for studio time. It was her way to give back to her community. She was a big supporter of the music and arts programs in the local city schools. If not for programs such as those, she would never have gotten her start.

"Why? What's going on?" Meg asked with wide eyes.

"I have a song I wrote, but I don't want anyone to hear it yet."

"Okay, no problem. I'll clear the house so that you can have a private session with your producer and recording engineer. You need anything else?"

Nina shook her head as they walked toward the studio, her thoughts deep in the lyrics that woke her up from her sleep. She had so many emotions running through her that she needed to let them out. She'd go crazy if she didn't. For her to wake in the middle of the night, she knew it was time.

Rose had called her that morning with the news that Luke had a new girlfriend. She turned on the television and found the news filled with word that Luke had moved on. All the gossip columns were in an uproar that he had a new girlfriend so quick after dumping Nina Hunt.

She cut it off and tried to ignore the information, but couldn't help going online to see who it was. Of course it was some swimsuit model. She rolled her eyes as she had stared at the picture. She would be a fool to say that she had gotten over him as quick as he seemed to have gotten over her.

Yes, it was time for her to express what was festering in her chest.

"No, I'm good," she growled as she opened the door. They walked into the building to the main recording booth, where there was a host of people hanging around. Normally, she wouldn't mind the company of extra singers to help lay vocals and musicians to record, but today, she didn't want to be interrupted.

"Today, the only people needed in this recording session is the producer and recording engineer. If your name is not Scott or Bill, you need to get out," Meg said as she walked into the room. The room fell quiet as they all looked at her. "We're serious. Out!"

Nina made her way over to Scott and Bill in the engineer room outside the booth. They turned to her as she sat in her chair.

She knew this was a unique request.

"What's going on, Nina?" Scott asked with his eyebrows raised.

She smiled at both of them. She pulled her iPad from her messenger bag.

"I have an idea." She paused as she watched the last person walk out of the studio. Meg gave her a thumbs-up as she closed the door. Nina knew that her sister would keep everyone out of the studio. Between Tank and Meg, no one would bother them until Nina said so.

"Must be serious." Bill laughed. He had worked as her recording engineer for years. She knew that she would be able to count on him for everything.

"I need to be honest with you. These songs we're working on won't be going out on my album for the record label," she stated. They both looked at her, shocked. "This will be an independent release, like how all the rappers are doing mix tapes independently. This will be my mix tape. I'm going to release it on the internet only."

"This is going to be fire." Scott nodded.

"I've already got my manager working with all the platforms to get it out there." She tucked her hair behind her ear, relieved that they would both be on her side.

"What have you got?" Scott nodded to her tablet. She could see that he was interested in what she was about to say.

She blew out a deep breath. It was now or never.

"As you know, with all the shit that Luke and I went through and the breakup, I've been writing." She looked at Scott, and the glint in his told her he knew exactly where she was going with this.

"Fast tempo or slow?" Scott asked, immediately jumping on the beat machine. That's why she loved Scott so much and worked with him every chance she could get.

"For this song, I want it up-tempo, yet gritty. Even with what I've got to stay, I want people to groove to it," she murmured, bringing up the lyrics.

Bill immediately began toggling buttons and setting up on the digital mixer. The board in front of them had what seemed like millions of buttons, and that's why she paid Bill what she did. He was a master of making her records sound authentic and clear. The mixing and mastering done by this man was genius.

They worked alongside each other to come up with a beat, but nothing was what she really needed.

"You know what? Here, listen to this one." Scott grabbed his laptop and typed in a few commands before the song began playing. The minute she heard the first few chords, she knew it was what she was looking for.

"Scott, you're a genius!" she exclaimed, jumping in her chair. "That's hot, and exactly what I was thinking in my head." She stood and took her iPad and entered the booth, but ran back out and grabbed a water bottle from the refrigerator. She needed to ensure that her throat didn't get too parched while she sang. This time, she entered the booth and closed the door, sealing all sound from the other room. She glanced over at Scott and Bill through the glass as they prepared for her.

This was her sanctuary. In this room, she could be herself. She placed her tablet on the stand near her and grabbed her earphones. Placing them over her ears, she waited for Scott and Bill to get ready for her. She looked down at the lyrics and knew that she would be pouring her heart out from her relationship with Luke out there.

She did a few warm-ups while she waited for the sign.

"*Do Re Mi Fa So La Ti Do,*" she sang. She paused,

cleared her throat, and took a sip of water before repeating the song.

"We're ready when you are." Scott's voice came through to her and she nodded, taking another quick sip. She was nervous. She hadn't let anyone see the lyrics and she wasn't going to change a thing. That's why she was doing this project independently, so she would have full control over her song.

The music came on and her body swayed, but she held up her hand and motioned for him to start again. Scott nodded and restarted the song, and this time, she was ready. She needed to hear it again so she knew when to come in, but with this beat, she knew it immediately.

"Here we go. Take two," Scott called out. Bill gave her the thumbs-up sign that he was ready.

The beat started again and she opened her mouth, the words flowing through her.

I saw the dishonesty in your eyes
Shallow you were
Can't handle a real woman
I should have seen the signs
But my blinders were on
Now they're off

"Another round on me," Kevin shouted to the bartender.

They were out at the local bar to watch the baseball game. Sports in Cleveland was a big deal, and everyone was there to support the baseball team. The crowd roared as one of the home team's player hit a home run. Even Sid got in on the yelling at the screen as the other players who had filled the bases each made their way home.

The bartender dropped off their beers. Tonight was a night for the guys to hang out. Sid helped Kevin carry the drinks back to their table. He needed this. Working with Nina the past two weeks had him strung tight. The sexual tension between the two of them should be illegal.

"Took y'all long enough!" Stan shouted, laughing as they passed out the drinks. "I thought we were going to have to send out a search party!"

"It's Friday night. There's no way my beer mug should be empty," Chet grumbled, taking his full mug from Sid.

"Well, blame Kevin. He was trying to get the bartender's number but she shot him down. He was practically begging over there," Sid joked, sitting down.

Hanging with the guys was always a blast. They tried to get together about twice a month, and usually during a game.

"Isn't that right, Sid?" Kevin laughed. Sid blinked and found all eyes on him.

"What?" he asked, bringing his beer to his lips.

"I said, the blonde over there has had her eyes on you since the minute we walked in. I said she's right up your alley."

He looked in the direction that Kevin pointed. Sure enough, a little skinny blonde whose boobs were definitely fake, blew him a kiss. Her face was caked with too much makeup.

He nodded to her, not trying to be an ass, but no, she wasn't what he wanted. Images of soft mocha skin came to mind. Hazel eyes, plump lips, and curves for days was what he wanted.

No, the blonde wasn't his type.

Not anymore.

"She's all right," he announced, turning back to the guys.

"Have you hit your head?" Garfield 'G' Jeffers, a friend of theirs since childhood asked. There was no way that G would let anyone call him by his government name. He had been in plenty of fights in the old neighborhood when someone called him Garfield.

"No, she's too skinny. I'm a big man. I need my woman to have some extra cushion." He smiled, joining in on the jokes.

"For the pushing," Chet shouted, raising his glass to Sid's. Sid chuckled at his friend, who was close to needing a ride home tonight. Looked like he was a few too many in his cups. "Now, Sid here is a man after my own heart. I've been trying to tell you all that for years. Skinny broads are not made for men like us."

"Here, here" they all agreed, clanking their beer mugs together.

The television closest to them was not showing the game, but instead, one of those gossip shows. Sid glanced up at the mention of Nina's name. There was a picture of her in a sexy, low-cut dress that stopped mid-thigh. His eyes were drawn to the man she had her arm entwined with—a tall, handsome, African American man who Sid had seen in a few movies. They made a handsome couple. The screen then showed two women in a studio, discussing Nina's breakup as if they were discussing sports.

"Looks like paradise is officially over for Nina Hunt," the woman on television announced. "Seems to me that she is officially single. So men, get ready for her."

They cut to video of Nina, dressed in a sexy outfit that showed lots of skin, leaning up against a black sports car, singing, as a rapper sat in the driver's seat, nodding his head to the beat. It cut to random pictures of her performing before going back to the women in the studio.

"It looks as if Luke Stow has officially moved on," the female on TV announced.

"Did you see with who? Swimsuit model, Becka Attaway." The other woman smiled.

"I still say Luke made a bad move. I mean, how can

you break up with Nina Hunt? Nina versus Becka? If I were a man, there would be no doubt in my mind Nina would be my choice," the first woman huffed. Sid nodded his head in agreement.

"Me too. But have you seen Nina lately? From what I've heard, she's now in the gym getting her breakup body together."

Sid had heard the term before. A breakup body was when the person would get themselves in shape to either make the ex jealous or to catch their rebound. His eyes flew back to the screen.

No, he didn't want to be her rebound.

He wanted her so bad. Her taste from their kiss was still on his tongue.

He didn't know about forever, but he knew he wanted to be her right now.

CHAPTER
six

"Ow, ow, ow," Nina cried out over a strong cramp in her leg. It was the worst cramp she had ever had. Her muscles balled up tight from her toes, all the way up into her groin. She lowered herself to the mat as Sid came over to her.

"What is it?" he asked, concern filling his eyes. In the past few weeks, he hadn't so much as touched her. Even when it was suggested that she get a massage, one of the masseuses performed it for her.

The sexual tension in the air was so thick, it could be cut with a knife. She'd faithfully come to every appointment, just to lust after her trainer.

"Oh my god. A cramp," she cried out, beating her fist on the mat as the pain became unbearable.

"Okay, hold on," he murmured as he knelt down on the mat beside her. He gently rolled her over to her back. "Which leg?"

"Right," she cried out again as he removed her shoe.

He began to massage her leg, starting at her calf muscle, murmuring soothing words to her as the tears flowed from her eyes. She covered them with her arm as his hands worked the knots from her leg. The pain began to lessen as he rubbed.

"I can feel it," he mused as his hands slid up her thigh, kneading her quad muscle. "It's a hard knot. Have you been drinking as much water as I suggested?"

"Yes!" she bellowed as he hit a sore part of her thigh.

"I'm sorry. It shouldn't take too much longer." He used a fist to push into her muscle and she gasped.

"Your supplements?"

"Yes," she moaned as he applied more pressure. As part of her weight loss journey, he had ensured that she was taking good vitamin supplements and drinking plenty of water.

Her body was waking up from the feel of his hands on her. She bit her lip as her nipples drew into tight little buds, straining against her sports bra. He ran his hands down her entire leg and began to massage her foot.

"Feel any better?" His voice lowered as he ran his thumb along the center of her foot.

"Yes." She held back a moan of pleasure. Massages were one of her weakness, and by the feel of his hands on her, he was a master at it. His hands began to make their way back up her leg, stopping at her calf muscle again.

She could feel the moisture begin to collect at the apex of her thighs.

Go up higher, she wanted to shout at him. Her body tingled everywhere from his hands.

As if reading her mind, his hands crept up higher, reaching her thigh again. Her thighs opened, inviting him.

She heard his quick intake of breath as he gripped her thigh tight. She just needed his hand to go over a few inches and he'd be right on the outside of her center.

"Nina," he whispered, his hand sliding to the left, massaging the part of her thigh where it met her pelvic bone.

Her back arched as he slid his hand over her center. She cursed that she still had on her leggings. As if knowing what she needed, his thumb connected with her sensitive nub through her pants and underwear. She was on the edge as she moaned, thrusting her pelvis against his fingers as he began massaging her clit.

"Sid, please," she groaned, throwing her arm away from her eyes so she could see him. His face was strained as he continued to tease her. Bracing himself over her, he pulled down her bra, exposing a single breast, still damp from her sweat. The nipple was pebbled, dark, and waiting for him.

"You're gorgeous," he murmured before leaning in to capture her freed mound in his mouth. She cried out as he licked her nipple, encircling it with his tongue. He sucked, licked, and nipped her, making the need for him rise in her chest. She gripped his head in her hands as her hips moved against his hand.

She wanted him deep inside of her. So deep, she wouldn't be able to breathe.

"Oh God, Sid, I'm almost there. Don't. Stop," she growled, not wanting him to leave her in this state. If he pulled away from her now, she would take violent measures against him. He clamped her nipple with his teeth before soothing it with his tongue. He pressed harder on her as she rocked her core against his hand.

"Let go, Nina," he ordered as she moaned loudly. He captured her mouth with his to silence her cries as her release took her over. Her body fell back against the mat as he removed his hand from her core and settled fully between her legs. She could feel his bulge against her as he deepened the kiss.

She didn't care who walked in on them.

His tongue swept into her mouth, tasting her. His kiss was consuming her as if he were a man taking his first drink of water. It was everything to her. She pulled him closer to her, her legs encircling him, drawing him closer to her. She rubbed her center against his thick length and wanted to feel him pushing into her.

"Not here." He broke the kiss, placing another one gently on her lips.

"I thought you wanted a platonic relationship." Clearly, his cock had other plans.

"I thought I could fight what I feel for you." He pulled his face back and brushed her hair from her face. Staring down at her, she saw desire and lust in his eyes. "I'm tired of fighting it."

"I want you," she whispered, and knew the words tumbling out of her mouth were true.

She wanted this man more than all the chocolate she had stashed in the nightstand in her bedroom. And anyone who knew her, knew not to get between her and milk chocolate.

"I want more than just fucking," he stated, seriousness taking over his features. "I don't want to be a rebound to your ex."

She paused as she looked at him. Is that what he'd thought this entire time? Never. She wasn't that type of woman. If she wanted a rebound, she would have just called up any A list actor who was single and arrange photoshoots out in public to make it seem like she had moved on. That was commonly done in the entertainment business to get notice in the media's eye.

"I don't think of you as a rebound," she admitted. She looked him in his eyes, and he studied her for a second before nodding, satisfied with her answer.

"Go out with me."

"Like a date?" she asked, her voice ending in a

squeak. It had been a long time since she had been on just a regular date. Nothing she ever did was regular anymore. It would feel good to be good ol' Nina.

"You do know what a date is, right?" he asked, standing from the floor. She missed the feel of his body covering hers. She took his outstretched hand and allowed him to help her up and stood erect, not needing to pretend to lose her balance. She quickly readjusted her sports bra to cover herself.

He pulled her to him, his hands on the small of her back. Her stomach clenched at the feel of him still rock hard against her stomach.

"Yes, I know what a date is," she scoffed.

"So, will you? A night on the town having fun? You'll love it, I promise." He turned his baby blues on her and she was a goner. She melted against him.

"Yes."

Sid blew out a nervous breath as he drove down the long driveway to Nina's house. He couldn't believe he was doing this. He had fought internally about his feelings for her. The past few weeks had been hell on his libido. He had walked around painfully aroused to the point that daily self-releasing his load while in the shower was doing nothing. Seeing her every day, hearing her laugh, being on the receiving end of her bad jokes left him wanting her even more.

Having her come apart in his arms was the final straw. A man could only take so much, and right now, he needed her more than the air he needed to breathe. If they had been anywhere else but the health club, he would have stripped their clothes from their bodies and dove balls deep into her sweet pussy.

She had asked him what to wear for their first date, and he insisted on jeans and anything with Cleveland's basketball team's logo on it. The season opener was tonight, and they would be joining his friends at his favorite bar, 4th Street Brewery. He knew how much she loved her hometown and missed it when away on tour.

He pulled up to the house and whistled. He figured that she owned a large house, but this thing was a mansion and screamed money. He parked the car and shut it off as thoughts raced through his head. He looked around the grounds, and every single acre screamed money.

But that's not Nina.

He didn't do bad for himself. He had gone to college, worked a job he absolutely loved, owned his own condo and had a savings. He was proud of his accomplishments in life, but looking at her home made it all feel so minuscule.

He couldn't back out now. Just the thought of seeing

Nina away from the gym had him hopping out of his Jeep. He jogged up the stairs and rang the doorbell before turning to look around.

The door opened, and a woman who shared a striking resemblance to Nina greeted him with a smile.

"Hello, can I help you?" She was polite, but he could see the confusion in her eyes.

"Hi, I'm Sid. I'm here for Nina—"

"I'm here," Nina gushed, grabbing the door.

His breath escaped his chest as if something slammed into it. She had pulled her hair into a high ponytail and let the dark curls fall behind her. Her makeup was light and barely noticeable. She wore a T-shirt with the basketball team's logo splashed across the chest. She must have tied it in the back because her navel was visible. Her jeans were tight with rips and holes in them. She had on killer heels that left him wanting to adjust himself, but he resisted. He didn't think it would be appropriate to be groping his cock in front of her and her family member.

"I think you broke him," the woman chuckled next to him.

"Hi," Nina murmured shyly.

"Hey." He smiled at her. "I'm Sid." He reached out his hand to the woman to introduce himself again.

"Hi, I'm Meg, Nina's sister." She smiled a real smile this time and took his hand.

"Are you ready?" he asked Nina, his eyes automatically going back to hers.

"Yes." She hugged her sister and stepped out of the house and onto the porch.

"Tank isn't going with you?" Meg asked with her eyebrow raised.

"He is, but he's staying back and will step in if we need him."

He turned to her, confused. Why would she need her bodyguard against him? They had been together plenty of times in the gym without the need for her bodyguard.

"Not against you. It's the public. Sometimes things can get a little crazy and Tank has to step in," she informed him. She moved closer and slid her hand into his.

She was a superstar. Music royalty. He had to remember that. It wasn't her needing protection from him, but the crazy public. He'd heard about crazed fans before and he'd be damned if he let anything happen to her on his watch.

"I won't let anything happen to you," he murmured, staring down into her eyes, drawing her closer.

"Okay, you two. Get out of here and have fun." Meg shooed them off the porch. He led Nina down the stairs and to the passenger side of his Jeep. He opened the door, helped her into the car and buckled her seat belt.

"You're such a gentleman." Her hand rubbed along the scruff of his jaw.

"Safety first," he murmured as he backed out and shut her door.

It was just good home training. His father would string him up by his toes if he wasn't a gentleman. That was just how he was brought up. Protect the female. Be the protector, the provider, and treat her as a partner. His mother definitely added that part on. These values were instilled in him and his younger brother, Mic. His father was the one that ensured that his boys grew up to be good men, and his sister, Aimee, would know what qualities to choose in a man.

His parents, Harry and Margo McFarland, had been married for forty years, and were still very much in love.

He jogged to his side of the Jeep and jumped in. He started the car and turned to Nina.

"Ready to have some good ol' fun?" he asked.

"Hell yeah."

CHAPTER
~seven~

Nina was a little nervous going out in downtown Cleveland. It had been a while since she just got to be Nina in her hometown. When she was with Luke, they had gone to all the Hollywood functions and countries all over the world, but he never wanted to come home with her. They both owned homes on both coasts and he always preferred his home to hers in Cleveland.

Luke loved the glamour and fame. She did too, but she always found herself homesick for Northeast Ohio.

"You nervous?" Sid asked, turning to her.

"Am I that readable?" She laughed.

"Well, your leg is bouncing a mile a minute." She glanced down at her leg and willed it to behave.

"I don't know why I'm so nervous. I perform before millions of screaming fans and my nerves don't get this bad." She shook her head as she watched the scenery go by.

"You'll be fine. Me and the guys won't let anything

happen to you, so just relax and try to have a good time."
He laid his hand on her thigh and her eyes flew to him.

She knew that Tank was following behind them, and he had been against her going on this date with Sid. He may be in charge of her security, but he wasn't in charge of who she dated. If she knew Tank, he would have men throughout the bar to increase security for her. He was always prepared and took the necessary security measures to ensure that she was safe.

"We're here. I'm going to valet with the opening game being tonight. Everyone is going to be downtown," he announced.

"Okay." She nodded and looked at the familiar bar as Sid pulled up in front of the valet. Sid got out of the car and she grabbed her clutch as another valet came to her side and opened the door.

Here we go, she thought.

She stepped out of the car to the sight of a young black valet who looked at her in shock.

"Close your mouth, honey. You might catch a bug," she joked with him.

He immediately straightened up and smiled. "Sure thing, Ms. Hunt. Welcome home."

Her heart melted. That was why she loved her town so much. It was a town that was extremely proud of those who made it big. Actors, sports stars, singers, artists, it didn't matter. Cleveland always stood behind their own.

"Thanks." She threw him a wink as she took Sid's outstretched hand.

"Friend of yours?" he asked, drawing her to him as they approached the entrance.

"No, a fan." She smiled as he opened the door and guided her in. The atmosphere in the bar was one of excitement and fun. She glanced around and saw smiles all around.

"What if your friends don't like me?" she asked, tugging on his hand.

"Don't worry about it. If you're with me, they'll love you." He pulled her close and tucked her under his arm as he guided her through the throng of people. She relaxed as she leaned into him. She would have a good time.

It took them a little while longer to make it through the crowd as fans stopped her to snap pictures with her. Sid was patient as he waited for her to speak to people and pose for pictures.

"Sid!" His name was called out by a few guys at a table. They finally made it through the crowd and arrived at the table his friends were sitting at. Their faces froze with surprise as she came to his side and took his hand.

She held back a laugh as their eyes dropped down to their entwined fingers.

"Nina, this is Kevin, he owns Unlimited Fitness.

This burly man with the beard that looks like birds could nest in it is Stan. To his left is Chet. You might have to watch him because he's a ladies' man. Then finally, this is G. Don't ever ask him his full name."

"Okay, *Sidney*," G coughed.

She nodded and smiled at each of them as they remained starstruck.

"Sidney?" she asked, turning to him.

"Long story," he groaned, flipping G the bird.

"Sid, you've been holding out big time!" Chet was the first to break the silence. They all laughed as Sid pulled out her chair for her before taking his seat beside her. Their table choice was perfect. They were tucked off in the corner in their own little world.

"Well, what can I say? I tried to resist, but she wouldn't take no for an answer," he joked.

She scoffed and slapped his arm with the back of her hand. The guys all chuckled at him, acting as if she hurt him.

Time flew too fast. Nina couldn't remember a time she'd laughed so hard and so much. She wiped a tear from her eye as they bantered back and forth while they all watched the game. Cleveland was winning, and Nina's night couldn't get any more perfect. She was just a little tipsy, but didn't care.

"Next round on me!" she shouted over the cheering

crowd. She'd noticed how the guys had been sharing the tab.

"You don't have to do that," Sid chuckled, laying a kiss on her forehead.

"Well, you brought me drinking with the guys and dammit, I'm going to pull my weight on the booze!"

"Now that's a woman for you," G hollered, raising his almost empty glass in the air.

"Here, here!" the others chimed in with glasses raised, laughing.

"I'll be back." She scooted her chair back and motioned for Sid to sit back down as he moved to go with her.

"I got it." She smiled. The crowd in the bar had finally calmed down after realizing she just wanted to hang out and watch Cleveland basketball.

She made her way through the crowd and spotted Tank sitting over by the bar. His eyes had been on her the entire time. He'd done as promised and stayed back, but she knew if anything would jump off, he'd bulldoze his way to her like a tank.

"Well, I'll be. Nina Hunt," the bartender greeted. Nina smiled at the overly excited guy, then laughed as he hopped on the bar, calling out for everyone's attention.

"What is he doing?" she muttered to herself.

"Hey, everyone! Can I have your attention? We have Cleveland's own, Nina Hunt, in the house! Now, Ms.

Nina, as the owner of 4th Street Brewery, I want to welcome you home from your long tour."

"Aww..." She sighed, her hands coming up to her heart. She waved at everyone and blew a few kisses as the bar broke out in cheers and whistles. Her vision blurred for a second as people began to chant her name.

"Nina! Nina! Nina!"

"And I'm sure everyone here agrees with me in saying that Luke Stow is an ass! You do you, and don't think twice about that asshole!"

The bar broke out into cheers of agreement as he jumped back down behind the bar.

"You're crazy!" she shouted over the noise. She glanced at the television behind the bar and saw the home team had just brought their lead up to ten points.

"Whatever you want is on the house tonight. Nina Hunt doesn't pay for anything here!" he shouted so that she could hear.

"I'm with some friends—"

"Friends of Nina's are friends of mine," he cut her off, smiling. "Rick Banner." He offered his hand to her.

She smiled as she shook his hand. "Well, Rick Banner, seeing as how you know me, I guess I don't need to tell you my name. And thank you."

She quickly ordered another round of beers for her and the guys. A waitress came around the bar with the order on a tray and ushered Nina away, carrying the tray behind. They arrived at the table and Nina helped pass out the beers.

"Thank you." Nina handed the woman a hefty tip for her troubles.

"No problem, Ms. Hunt," the girl gushed as she scurried away.

"I missed you," Sid said as she moved to take her seat. He grabbed her by her waist and pulled her onto his lap.

"I wasn't gone that long," she exclaimed as the guys showed their approval of them. She was excited that his friends seemed to like her, and she liked the crazy bunch as well.

She laughed as she settled on him and instantly noticed his hard member underneath her bottom. The bar slowly faded away as she stared into his hooded eyes. Her breath caught in her throat at the feel of his fingers drawing little circles on the exposed skin on her lower back.

"Mr. McFarland, is that a beer glass in your lap or are you just happy to see me?" she murmured into his ear. She nipped his lobe with her teeth and drew back slightly as a shudder passed through him. She could feel his breath on her lips as she stared into his eyes.

"Oh, I'll be very happy to see you later tonight," he replied.

"Really?" She leaned in to meet his lips in a searing kiss. It wasn't hard, but it was hot, short, and sweet. She pulled back, her body practically trembling with need. She leaned her forehead against his, trying to catch her breath.

"Do you really need to see the last of the game?" he asked, pressing his jean covered cock against her. She held back a moan as she could feel her body growing slick with need.

"Hell no. I'm recording it as we speak."

"Let's go."

Sid drove like the flames of hell were after him. Thankfully, there was a freeway near the bar that he was able to jump on to take them back to Nina's house.

"Thank you." Nina's soft voice broke the silence.

"For what?" he asked, looking over at her. She leaned over and grabbed his free hand and entwined their fingers.

"For treating me like I'm normal, and taking me out on a normal date to have a good time."

"What do you mean normal? Just because you're a superstar, you're not allowed to just go out and have fun?" he asked.

That sounded like a sad excuse of a life. He couldn't imagine not being able to go out with his friends. He had saw Tank sitting at the bar and a few other meatheads that usually weren't in the brewery. They probably worked for Tank. He felt almost sorry that for her to go out, it had to be an entire security production just so she could have a little bit of fun.

"Most people expect me to be this glamorous person all the time. Everyone is so fake in Hollywood, and even in the music scene. That's why I've always kept my house here. When I'm here, I can just be Nina. I don't have to be *the* Nina Hunt that everyone expects me to be."

He tightened his grip on her hand, not wanting to let her go. Deep down, he wanted to protect her from the world, but knew that there wouldn't be a thing he could do. What he did know was that tonight, he would make her feel special. He didn't know how much time he would have with her, but he would make the most of it.

Twenty minutes later, they were pulling into her long driveway. The ride to her house was comfortable. They spoke of their childhoods and where they grew up. During the short car ride, they had learned so much about each other.

"Park in front of that garage."

He guided his Jeep where she directed him. Cutting off the engine, and glanced down at their still entwined hands.

"Are you sure about this?" he asked, gently rubbing her hand with his now free one. He needed to know for sure before they took this step. Letting her dry hump his hand was one thing, but this was taking their relationship to another level. If she changed her mind, he would leave, no questions.

"Yes," she breathed. In the dark truck, he could see her wide eyes and knew she wanted him as much as he wanted her.

With a growl, he exited the vehicle and made his way around to open her door. Helping her down from the truck, he looked down at her high heels as she led him to the house and shook his head.

How did women walk in those things?

CHAPTER
eight

He followed her through the quiet mansion, seeing touches of her throughout the house. He could tell she didn't hire a decorator. No, Nina picked out every single piece of furniture and painting.

This was her home.

"Do you live here by yourself?" he asked as she led him up a flight of stairs.

"No, Meg lives with me. Her room is in the other wing. When I bought this house, I wanted my own private quarters, so her room and guest rooms are located on the other side of the house, away from me. Here I get all the privacy I want."

They reached the upper level, but instead of looking around at the hallway, his eyes were drawn to her ass in her snug jeans. She looked over her shoulder and giggled before stopping at a door that was closed and turned to lean her back against it. A shy look came over her as she stared up at him.

He growled as he stepped closer to her, covering her mouth in a bruising kiss. His cock was painfully pushing against his jeans. She gasped and his tongue dove inside her mouth, a hint of beer still lingered on her tongue. Her fingers made their way to his hair, fisting it tight.

He reached for the handle and turned it. She giggled as they almost fell to the floor when the door opened.

"Funny, huh," he said playfully before reaching down to pick her up in his arms.

"Sid!" she exclaimed, wrapping her arms around his neck.

"I've got you." He could see that she truly had her own quarters up here. They were standing in what looked to be a lounge, with plush couches and television setup on the wall. It was like a family room inside of her room. A black piano sat in the corner in front of the windows, and he could easily imagine her lounging on the couch, watching the basketball games or a movie there. "Lead the way."

"That door over there is my bedroom."

He walked past the larger couch in the direction she had pointed. Gently pushing the door open with his foot, the moonlight flowed into the room through her floor-to-ceiling windows.

"No curtains?" he asked, eyebrow raised.

"No. No one can see into the room because I had the

windows tinted. It's a beautiful view, and it would be a shame to cover it up with curtains."

He gently placed her down on the bed. She tried to sit up, but he pushed her down.

"Relax," he murmured, wanting to undress her himself. She hesitated at first, but then relented and laid back on the bed. He gently took off her heels, massaging each foot. She moaned as he kneaded the arches.

He reached up and unbuttoned her jeans and slid them down her legs. Tossing them over his shoulder, he looked down at the small scrap of material that posed as panties.

"I want to take your clothes off too," she murmured.

"You'll get your turn soon enough." He ran his hands along her soft caramel skin. He had imagined these legs naked since the first time they'd met, and he wanted to savor this moment. This was better than fucking Christmas. No gift would ever compare.

His hands made their way up to her panties and peeled them off, realizing they had a problem. It was too dark in the room. He wanted to see everything. He looked around and found a lamp on the bedside table. He flicked the lamp on, casting them in soft light.

"What are you doing?" she asked, sitting up on her elbows. He reached for his wallet and set it on the nightstand. He reached for her again, this time wanting to see her completely naked in front of him. He pulled her shirt over her head and tossed it aside. His breath escaped his chest as he took in the sheer black bra that covered her breasts. The sheerness did nothing to hide her dark areolas. He gently reached out and unsnapped the clasp that was nestled between them.

He hissed as he took in her bare breasts. He covered her mounds with both his hands, loving how each one filled them to capacity. He squeezed and rolled her nipples between his fingers. They were just as he liked—soft, supple, and large.

"Sid, you have on too many clothes." He ran his fingertips along her skin before pushing her legs apart to find her glistening pussy lips staring back at him, calling his name.

He leaned down and began to feast on Nina's sweet-smelling pussy. She cried out as he licked, taking his full taste of her. He wanted more. She tasted so sweet. Her hips thrust forward as she cried out his name.

He loved hearing his name on her lips.

He wanted to savor this moment. Her hips bucked against him, her head thrashing around on the bed as he slipped not one finger, but two, inside of her tight channel.

Her fingers fisted his hair as she rode his face. He focused his attention on her tiny bundle of nerves, ignoring the pain from the tight grip she had on his hair. He wanted to make sure she reached her release. She would need the extra moisture to take him. In the back of his mind, he knew that they would be a perfect fit, even though she was so much smaller than him.

"Oh, God. Sid," she cried out as he pumped his fingers inside of her. He clamped down on her clit and she exploded. A scream tore from her as her body tensed. Her release coated his fingers as her muscles clamped down on him. He refused to let up on her as she rode out the waves of her orgasm.

He was nowhere near done with her.

Her body flopped down on the bed, her chest moving at a fast pace. He stood up and pulled his T-shirt over his head, his eyes locked on her naked form. Deep down, he was pleased that he caused her such an intense orgasm. He pushed his jeans and boxer briefs down, freeing his throbbing cock. He kicked his shoes and clothing the rest of the way off and reached for his wallet, pulling out the gold foil package. He ripped it open and quickly sheathed himself.

Her eyes opened as he pulled her to the edge of the bed. Did she know how beautiful she was? He agreed with the owner of the bar, her ex was an ass, but he was glad the other man had left. If not for Luke Stow, he would have never met Nina Hunt.

"I need you, Sid," she whimpered as he spread her legs again.

"You got me," he growled as he drove his cock into her. She released a drawn-out moan as he was finally seated balls deep inside of her. He paused, cursing at how tight her pussy was. The slickness from her release allowed him to slip easily into her, but her walls were snug around him.

He had to move or he wouldn't last long.

She shifted her hips as he pulled back and surged forward again.

Hard.

She shouted as he began to thrust, unable to control himself anymore. She met him for every thrust. The expression on her face was of pure pleasure.

He gripped her legs and pushed them back toward her, opening her to him even more. He couldn't take his eyes off his cock disappearing into her greedy little pussy. It had to be one of the most erotic sights he'd ever seen.

He could feel the contractions of her orgasm as her pussy pulsated around him.

"Fuck. Nina!" he roared as he followed her, coming hard. His knees drew weak as he continued to thrust into her hot core, her pussy milking him for all he was worth.

Her moans and his gasps for air filled the room until neither of them could move. His heart raced as he slowly pulled out of her. He crawled into the bed and braced himself over her. She opened her eyes, meeting his stare, and he leaned down to kiss her.

Nina could be addicting, and he couldn't think of anything else he'd rather be addicted to. She didn't hold back in the kiss, her tongue meeting his as he tasted her.

"Will you stay with me tonight?" she asked. Her eyes searched his, as if trying to find the answer to her question.

"Yes."

Nina leaned her head against her hand as she lay next to Sid, watching him sleep. She had no regrets of their night together. She was deliciously sore between her legs, and couldn't ever remember a time when she was fully sated from a night of lovemaking.

Never.

As he slept, she stared at him, taking in his tan skin and the stubble on his jaw. How she loved the feel of the rough hair on the inside of her thighs. A shiver coursed through her body with just the thought of Sid's face between her legs again.

She sighed as she continued her assessment of him. His face was relaxed as he slept. She glanced over at the clock and saw it was a little after six in the morning. She didn't think he had to work at the club this weekend. She had finally graduated to where she didn't have to go every day. As she stared at him, she could see the lyrics of a song come to mind. It was like a movie playing out in front of her eyes.

Sid.

The song would be about him. She felt a rush to get the emotions written so she quietly slipped from the bed. Grabbing her silk robe, she wrapped it around herself and quietly walked from the room and into her lounge, picking up her tablet from the couch on her way over to her piano.

She sat on the bench as the words flowed from her. She began to type out each word as they flowed from her heart. Within ten minutes, she had the hook down too. She smiled. She was happy that not only did she have her pain to get through, but happiness she wanted to share with the world.

She placed her fingers on the keys of the piano and began to think of the music she wanted to go with the lyrics she had just written.

Closing her eyes, she began to play, letting her fingers glide along the ivory keys as she began to sing her song from the heart.

I can tell by the way you look at me

That you want me.
I smile,
you smile.
I want you.
I need you.
You bring me joy.
No matter what anyone says,
you make me smile.
You fill me with joy.

She paused her song as her fingers continued to fly across the keys until she paused. She was pleased with what she had so far. It was the perfect summary of their meeting and their relationship so far. She would add this song to her independent album, being one of the last songs.

The album would be a representation of what she had been going through the last few months. She knew the media would go crazy once she released it, but she didn't care. She had yet to speak to Luke since he walked out on her, but she didn't need or want to talk to him. He had made it very clear that he didn't want her any longer.

"Wow."

She jumped, not hearing Sid walk into the room.

She smiled a shy smile, embarrassed that she was caught singing her heart out to an empty room.

"Morning. I didn't mean to wake you," she chuckled.

She noticed that he had put his boxer briefs back on. Her eyes took in his full form in just his underwear, and thought that it was a pure crime for this man to ever cover his body with clothes.

"That was beautiful. I'm not complaining to be awakened by a beautiful sound such as that." He smiled as he came around the piano. Leaning down, he pressed his lips to hers in an early morning kiss.

"Did you sleep well?" she asked as she stood. He wrapped her in his arms.

"I did, but this beautiful woman that welcomed me into her bed and shared her body with me, disappeared by the time I woke up," he murmured against her head.

"Really? That was rude of her. She just disappeared?" she joked, smiling against his chest. She loved the feel of his warm, hard chest against her cheeks. It was solid muscle. She ran her fingers down his abdomen, unable to resist. His stomach shook from laughter.

Someone was ticklish.

"This view is beautiful," he gushed as he guided them to the windows. It was one of the reasons she bought the house. The floor-to-ceiling windows allowed her to connect with nature from the comforts of her home, with the perfectly manicured landscape as the perfect backdrop. He turned her in his arms and rested his chin on the top of her head.

"It's one of my favorite parts of the house," she

confided, captivated by two deer scampering along her back yard without a care in the world. She tilted her head to the side as he laid a kiss along the side of her neck.

She moaned as he nipped her skin gently as he began untying her robe.

"You said these windows are tinted?" he asked as he pushed her robe to the floor, leaving her naked.

"Yes," she hissed as he brought her flush against him. His hand slid down to her almost flat stomach to her swollen labia, exposing her clit. She moaned as he circled it with his finger. Her nipples beaded from the chilled air caressing them and her breasts grew heavy, needing to feel his calloused hands on them.

"Have you ever been fucked for all the world to see?" he asked, his voice a low whisper in her ear. Her stomach clenched at the thought of someone watching them together. He dipped his finger into her, her slickness coating him.

"No," she groaned as she rode his hand.

"Hmm...You want the world to see me fuck you, don't you?" He teased her, running his finger across her sensitive flesh. She wasn't going to last long.

She just didn't understand how her body was always two seconds from detonating around him.

"Please," she moaned as he pinched her little hidden nub of flesh. "Sid!" she screamed as she exploded.

His dirty talk and finger was the only thing she needed to get off. He caught her body against his and felt him tug his shorts off. He sat down on the bench and turned her toward him, his stiff member standing at attention, waiting for her to impale herself on him.

"Come here, my little songstress. Ride me."

CHAPTER
~nine~

Monday morning had come faster than Sid had liked. Today, he had given Nina the day off. They had spent the entire weekend together. They took advantage of the beautiful weather on Sunday and spent the entire day outside.

Now, here it was Monday, and he was back at work. Nina had an important meeting today, and promised to call him when she could. He hoped her day was going good. She had been excited. All he knew was that it had to do with her upcoming album.

He shook his head and laughed at himself. Here he was daydreaming over a woman, as if he were a school boy with his first crush. He pulled up the spreadsheets he needed to work on, becoming engrossed in his work until the phone on his desk rang, jarring him from his thoughts. He snatched it up to answer it.

"Hello?"

"Yes, can I have Sidney McFarland please?" He

paused his typing at the use of his full name. Everyone who really knew him, knew he didn't go by his government name.

"Who is this?" he asked suspiciously. He paused and grabbed the phone in his hand.

"This is Samantha Roberts with the Cleveland Gazette. We have video footage and photographs of you getting quite cozy with Nina Hunt. Would you care to comment on your relationship with Ms. Hunt?" the voice rushed out.

"What? No, I don't want to comment." He slammed the phone down into its base. Running a shaky hand across his face, he blew out a long breath.

The phone rang again.

"Hello?" he answered, dread filling his chest.

"Hi, is this Sidney McFarland?" a voice asked.

"Who is this?" he snapped, anger beginning to mount in him at the invasion of his privacy.

"Yes, this is Roxy with the Hot List—"

He didn't give Roxy a chance to finish her sentence. He instantly picked the phone up and dialed out to the reception area.

"Hey, Sid." Ivy's chipper voice came onto the line.

"Have you transferred calls back to me?" he growled.

"Um, no, I haven't. Is everything okay?" she asked, sounding worried.

"Yeah. Any calls that come through in regards to

Nina Hunt need to be ignored. No one is to give away any information about her. "

"Of course, Sid. I'll make sure anyone else who may answer the phone knows to say no comment like they do in the movies."

"Thanks, Ivy."

Shit.

He pulled out his cell phone from the top drawer of his desk and swiped the glass screen.

The desk phone rang again. He eyed it, but knew that he couldn't just ignore it.

"Hello!" he snapped.

"Hi, can I have Sidney McFar—"

He slammed the phone down again. This time, he didn't wait for the person to finish their sentence.

He sent a quick text to Kevin to let him know what was going on and to call him on his cell phone before pulling Nina's number up. He hit her name, placing the phone by his ear as it rang. He stood from his desk and began to pace the office.

Ring. Ring. Ring.

Her voicemail picked up. He sighed and listened to the generic pre-recording.

"Hey, Nina. It's me. Call me." He hung up the call, unsure of what to do next. He knew that she had a meeting and would be unavailable. He didn't know what to make of the media.

There was a brisk knock at the door. He looked over and saw Ivy standing in the doorway.

"Sid, you're all over the news," she announced.

"What?" he asked in disbelief.

Why the hell would he be on the news?"

"Look on the internet. It's all over the media sites."

"What's all over the media sites?" He moved back to his desk and pulled up the internet, and sure enough, there he was.

A picture of Nina walking toward the bar holding his hand. Another of her tucked under his arm. There were pictures of them from their night at the bar. Someone had snapped a picture of her on his lap, their faces close, and one while they were sharing a kiss.

Shit.

"I didn't know that you two were dating!" Ivy exclaimed, jumping in place.

"We've only been on one date," he mumbled as his eyes began to read through the article.

He grew angry with the invasion of privacy. Those people had no right to photograph them and turn around and sell them to the media.

How dare they!

"Oh, well, you two make a beautiful couple." Ivy smiled, moving to close the door. "We'll hold the phones down. I'm not sure how the calls have been coming back to you though. Seems like your backline number got out somehow."

The phone rang again and he growled as he snatched it up from the base.

"What?" he snapped.

"I hope you don't answer the phone like that all the time," Kevin's scolded.

"My bad." He sighed, running a hand through his hair.

"Dude, it's all over the radio about you and Nina. Apparently, you're Nina's new beau," Kevin chuckled.

"That's what I'm hearing," he grumbled as he clicked on another story, citing that Nina had gotten over Luke and moved on with a local guy.

"Have you spoken to her today?"

"No, she had some big meeting today. I just tried to call her and her voicemail picked up."

"Don't let all this fame go to your head." Kevin laughed.

"This isn't funny," he growled into the phone. "This is an invasion of her privacy and mine."

"Well, I hate to break it to you, but nothing is ever private for a celebrity," Kevin said, all joking vanishing from his voice. "Looks like you have a decision to make. Continue whatever relationship you've started with her, or...you know."

Sid knew what Kevin was getting at, but he didn't

want to admit it. He could take whatever the media threw at him. He just didn't want her to have to go through another storm because of him. It was bad enough she was still the talk in gossip magazines and television shows because of the idiot dumping her. Now they would be talking about her again because of him.

"Or what?" he asked, looking up at the ceiling.

"Walk away."

Walk away from Nina?

His Nina?

Nina, who he loved watching fall apart in his arms?

Not a chance in hell he was walking away.

Nina jogged up the stairs to her private jet. Pride always filled her chest when she thought of how she owned her own private plane. It was a luxurious vehicle that allowed her to travel all over the world in privacy. It could seat a little over twenty people, which came in handy for touring around the world. She spoiled her band, and they all traveled with her on this plane.

The open cabin allowed for swivel plush armchairs, and even two leather couches for relaxation. It was the ultimate luxury and had come in handy with all the traveling she did.

She had flown to New York that morning to meet

with some of the executives of the platforms she would be releasing her secret album on. Her day had went as planned. Every platform agreed to distribute her independent album, and not only sell it, but let her take over. When her album released, her face would be everywhere.

She planned to take over the music industry. It was good to be the top selling female of all time. She hadn't even given them a date yet. They just knew that her people would contact them with the release date when she was ready.

"Nina, you were amazing," Tasha Goode announced as everyone settled into the plush leather seats of the jet. Tasha had been Nina's manager for the last eight years, and they had a great working relationship. The minute Nina approached her with the idea of an independent project, Tasha instantly jumped to work without needing prompting.

"You had them eating out of your hands." Meg laughed.

"Hard work pays off." Nina smiled as she kicked off her heels and stretched. It had been a long day of meetings.

The stewardess gained everyone's attention to let them know that the plane would be taking off shortly.

"Our girl deserves everything they were offering," Tank commented.

"Damn straight she does. Shit, she'll probably break the internet with this album. It's nothing like she's ever done before," Meg insisted.

"I'm just leaving my cards on the table. Everyone wants to know about what happened with me and Luke, and I'm going to tell my side of the story and that's it. No interviews about him, no nothing. My comments will be for them to go listen to the album," Nina chuckled.

"Hey, we may have a problem," Tasha announced, her eyes narrowed on her phone. She swiveled in her chair to turn toward Nina.

"What's wrong?" Nina sat up straighter in her chair, not liking the sound of Tasha's voice. Her manager always remained cool, and Nina could always count on her to handle whatever problems arose.

"I got a text from Rose. The media is in a frenzy now. She said today has been crazy."

"What now? Let me guess, Luke has another girl-friend?" She threw her head back against the supple leather headrest. Her eyes rolled so far back, they almost got stuck. She couldn't wait for this cloud that hung over her named Luke to move on.

How could she get over him when everyone kept throwing him in her face?

A rugged face appeared in her thoughts with baby blue eyes, and dark stubble on his jaw.

Sid.

"Turn the television on," Tasha called out as the plane jerked and began rolling toward the runway.

"I got it," Meg replied, grabbing the remote near her and aiming it at the television. Seconds later, it came on. She flicked through the channels as the plane took off at great speeds down the runway, and finally came to one of the popular channels where the show the Hot List ran.

"Looks like we're just in time," Tasha murmured as the still images of Nina appeared on the screen.

"Nina Hunt is on fire! Have you seen her body?" a voice spoke while they moved to different pictures of her out and about. "Luke who? Royalty songstress Nina Hunt has officially got her breakup body." The voice laughed.

The screen cut to a room full of reporters sitting around, talking and joking.

"What I love the most is that she kept her curves," one of the young black male reporters chuckled before looking into the camera. "Nina, call me."

Nina rolled her eyes as chuckles filled the room as the guy wiggled his eyebrows at the camera.

"I'm sure Luke Stow is thinking twice now about dumping her," a female stated, shaking her head. The group laughed and continued to banter back and forth.

Nina usually didn't watch these shows. The paparazzi were everywhere, and she never wanted to see what they actually spun in their articles or television shows.

The Hot List was one of the more popular shows for gossip, where a team of reporter met and discussed the latest gossip in the entertainment world. They had photographers in nearly every major city, professional and amateurs who always seemed to know where every celebrity was.

This wasn't the first time Nina had been mentioned on this show, and she was sure it wasn't going to be the last.

"Ugh, turn it," Nina groaned as the group made crude remarks about her weight loss and her sexiness.

"They at least got one thing right, you are looking good," Tank chuckled from his seat. "I'm proud of how hard you've been working."

The murmurs of agreement that went around the plane had her cheeks warming. Her team was the best and she couldn't imagine anyone else with her.

"Honestly, I didn't do it because of Luke, I did it for me. I wanted to get healthy. Touring takes a toll on my body, eating at all times of the day and night. No sleep, performing, and the traveling around the world doesn't give me time to think of my health. Since starting this journey, this is the best I've felt in a long time."

Meg paused on the Black News Network and shushed everyone as they too were talking about Nina.

Dread filled Nina because she knew the show Hot Off the Press never held any punches. It was a show with black comedians who discussed the latest gossip. The cabin of the jet drew quiet as everyone turned their attention to the show.

"Nina Hunt and some mysterious white guy?" The comedian, Lil Mike, laughed. "What the hell did Luke Stow do that was so bad that would leave Nina Hunt to run to the white man?"

Nina swallowed hard as she felt her team members glance at her. She'd been on television shows with Lil Mike and he never bit his tongue. He didn't care who he was interviewing; if something was on his mind, the whole world would know it.

"Here, I'll turn it—" Meg murmured, but Nina held her hand up and cut her off. She wanted to hear what people were saying. She'd been in the business a long time, and she had developed thick skin over the years.

Her eyes remained glued to the screen as the four comedians laughed while sitting around their table.

"Maybe she needs a break from black men in general. Let me tell you something. Let me find a good looking white man who wanted to pour some cream in my coffee, I'd snatch his ass up in a heartbeat," Grace Lee commented. She was a popular comedian known for her crude sex-infused comedy.

"Have you seen the pictures of them together?

97

Whoever this hunky man is, is definitely digging our Nina," another comedian Nina was unfamiliar commented.

They flashed to pictures of Nina and Sid's night at the bar. Someone had taken a massive amount of photos. There were photos of Nina tucked under Sid's arm, her on his lap, the kiss they shared, and them leaving the bar with their arms around each other.

"Okay, I understand she got her new body and is looking sexier than ever, but why a white guy? You trying to tell me that just because Luke Stow is an ass, that knocks out any other black guy?" the other male comic asked, causing the other cast members to share a chuckle.

"Exactly!" Lil Mike shouted, throwing his arms up in the air. "You know how many brothers were lining up to take a chance at Nina now that Luke is out the picture?"

"Cut it off," Nina snapped, her anger rising. The television screen went black as she turned her plush recliner toward the window of her private jet. Light gray clouds filled the air as night approached. She stared out the window, looking at the wings of the plane as it cut through the seemingly calm sky.

She just didn't get the media. She gets dumped and they are all in an uproar to get the story and find out the details of what went wrong between her and Luke.

She wasn't sure what this was between her and Sid. It was still new, and the glow from their magical weekend together had officially faded thanks to the media trying to study it under a microscope.

So what that he was white and she was black. This wasn't the first time an interracial couple had come together. This had been going on since the beginning of time. She ran a shaky hand through her straight hair and blew out a deep breath.

How was race even a problem now?

CHAPTER
Ten

Silence filled the cabin as everyone waited on her response. She bit her lip, pissed at the world right now. She should be able to date whoever she wanted. Who were they to dictate that she should stick with black men? She could think of plenty of black men in the entertainment business or not, who had wives and significant others who were not black, and it seemed to be more acceptable.

How was it different for a black woman to have relations with a white man? Why would she be ridiculed on finding companionship with someone outside of her race?

"What do you want us to do?" Tasha asked, jumping back into her managerial role.

"We're not putting out a statement of any kind. I'm not going to address any of the rumors or gossip that they're putting out there." Nina shook her head. It was none of the public's business who she dated.

"But are you seeing that guy? That's your trainer, right?" Tasha asked.

"I told Nina this would be a problem," Tank chuckled.

"Not now, Tank," she snapped. She didn't need this from her own people. He sat back in his chair and crossed his arms in front of him.

"Yes, Sid is my trainer and I really like him. He really likes me." She tucked her hair behind her ear as she thought of Sid. She was sure he had probably heard of the news stories floating around. She groaned as she thought of how the media had probably already tried to contact him. "At least he did before all of this." She waved at the television.

They fell into a silence. Nina's brain was running a mile a minute, trying to think of what she should do.

"So, how was it?" Meg's voice broke the strained silence.

"How was what?" Nina turned to her sister, confused.

"You know, being with a white guy?" A smile spread across her face.

"Meg!" Nina scoffed, feeling her cheeks warm at the question. Chuckles filled the room and Nina could feel all eyes on her.

"This is something I don't need to hear," Tank announced, getting up from his seat and heading to the back room of the plane. Her private jet included a bedroom with a wash room in the back. Aside from short trips around the country, she used her jet for international travel too. There was nothing like traveling in stylish luxury.

"Don't think I didn't notice that his Jeep was still parked in the driveway the next morning after your date." Meg cocked an eyebrow at her as she waited. Only her sister would call her out. Tasha chuckled as she settled back in her chair.

"No comment." Nina shook her head.

She wasn't one to kiss and tell. Her night with Sid had been amazing. She had never been so sexually satisfied after one night. It left her wanting him even more. She hated that she had to leave to go off to New York. If she would have had her way, she would have locked him in her room, handcuffed to her bed.

"Back to business, ladies. As much as we would all like to know the answer to the question, Nina's not giving up the details." Tasha chuckled. "So no press release. Ignore the press. Do what we normally do."

"Yes. I'm not responding to anything. It's none of their business," Nina said.

"You know this was the first time you were seen in public and I think they're just shocked. What we need to do is put you out in the public more. This was supposed to be your hiatus now that you're done with the tour, but instead, you decided to do an indie project. We can use the momentum of all this publicity, the good and the bad, to build up for your secret release."

Nina knew her manager was officially planning, but Tasha was right. The gossipers would continue talking and they could use it to their advantage.

She just wanted to focus on finishing her indie project and get back home. Her night out with Sid had given her a taste of what she had been missing— simple living and enjoying life.

She wearily looked at Tasha, who was deep in thought.

Shit, she was planning. Nina could see it in her face.

"What do you have in mind?" Nina asked, adjusting her dress.

"I'm sure you won't want to include Sid—"

Nina shook her head immediately.

"And that's fine. I would actually advise that you don't. But you do know they have the Writer's Guild Dinner coming up and you need to be there. They have you nominated for writer of the year and a few other awards. We can use events like this to draw attention to just you. They can keep playing off Luke, but at least it's on you."

Tasha was a genius, and she could protect Sid from the media. She nodded her head. She would do it. The Writer's Guild Dinner was a big deal. All the news media outlets covered it, there would be a red carpet and formal attire was required. It would be a great opportunity to show the industry that she was strong and wouldn't let a breakup tear her down.

"I'll do it. I remember getting the invitation, so let them know that Nina Hunt will be in attendance."

Sid couldn't concentrate on anything. It was getting late and he still hadn't heard from Nina. He knew once he got home, he wouldn't want to watch television. He didn't want to know what was being said in the media, so he decided for once to clean his house from top to bottom. Not that he was a dirty man, but cleaning was never one of his top priorities.

He'd worked up quite a sweat, but it paid off. His place was now officially spotless and smelled fresh.

Unlike him.

He trudged into his bedroom, stripping off his clothes and headed into the bathroom. He flipped the shower on and waited for the water to adjust to the right temperature. It was cold enough to freeze his balls off and he would prefer for that not to happen.

His thoughts turned to Nina.

He couldn't wait to hear the sound of her voice, to see her smile. He wanted to comfort her from the media backlash of them being together. He didn't care about the color of their skin, only how well they fit together when he was deep inside of her and how soft she felt against his hard muscles.

He stepped into the shower, trying to keep the erotic images from his mind. His cock stiffened with the thought of diving back between her soft thighs. He hurried through his shower, refusing to give in to the temptation of relieving himself with memories from their time together.

He finished toweling off as he walked back into his bedroom. Grabbing a pair of clean pajama pants, he threw them on when the sound of his cell phone ringing filled the air. He snatched it up, seeing Nina's name splashed across the screen.

"Hello," he answered.

"Hey." Her sultry voice came through the line, his cock instantly stiff.

"Hey yourself," he murmured, sprawling across his oversized king bed. He ran a hand across his chest, conjuring her face in his mind.

"What are you doing?" she asked.

"Waiting to hear from you. How are you holding up?" he asked, not beating around the bush. He was sure she had heard the media's stories.

"I'm fine. The media can talk all they want. It's part of the business, and one has to have thick skin. I just don't want them to bother you. You shouldn't have to deal with this mess."

"Don't worry about me. They'll forget about me soon enough. It's you I'm worried about," he admitted, his hand pausing on his chest.

Her quick intake of breath sounded in his ear.

"Sid?"

"What is it, baby?" he asked gently. He imagined her teeth catching her bottom lip as she did when she was deep in thought. He held back a groan as his cock painfully pushed against his pants.

"You're just too good to be true." She laughed softly. "Usually, people are vying for their fifteen minutes of fame and you're acting like a pro with it."

"I'm not like most people. The spotlight isn't for me."

"What is for you?" she asked, her voice dropping low.

"You," he answered her without hesitation.

"Open your front door."

He jumped from his bed and flew down the stairs, his heart hammering against his chest.

She was here.

He moved to the front door and flipped the porch light on. He snatched the door open to find her getting out the back seat of a black luxury vehicle. Tank was standing outside of it and shut the door, giving Sid a slight nod of his head as he walked back around the car to the driver's seat.

Sid could see that there were two women in the car, but his eyes were locked on Nina as she walked up the walkway. Her hips swayed in a flowing dark dress the hung off her shoulder, flowing around her calves. His mouth watered at the sexy brown skin that was on display. When did shoulders ever get sexy? He had no clue, but Nina's were sexy as hell.

Her high heels put her sexy calves on display as they moved toward him. He ended the call and tossed his phone onto his couch as she flew up the stairs and straight into his arms.

His hands immediately cupped her face and brought it up so he could cover her lips with his. She parted them and his tongue dove inside so he could taste her. She pressed closer to him as the kiss deepened. He took a few steps back into the house with her following him, pushing the door shut so he could push her up against it.

Her purse and phone dropped to the floor, but neither of them cared.

"I missed you," she gasped as he broke away to trail kisses along the side of her face and down to her neck.

"I missed you too," he muttered against her softness. His hands ran down her sides and disappeared beneath her dress. She gripped him by his hair and pulled his face back to hers, demanding another kiss. He was happy to oblige her. His fingers connected with the edge of her panties and pulled until he heard the beautiful sound of them ripping.

"Sid," she gasped.

"You don't need these around me," he muttered, dead serious. He glanced down into her eyes and meant it. He wanted to always have full access to her, especially when she looked this good. He would prove to her that she belonged to him. They were good together and he'd make her see it.

No other man would be able to follow him.

His cock pushed against her stomach to prove a point. A sensual grin spread across her face as he tossed her mangled panties over his shoulder. He trailed a finger over her bare mons pubis.

He parted her labia and stroked her sensitive hidden nub.

"Are you going to wear panties around me?" He nipped her bottom lip as she threw her head back against the door.

"Fuck!" she cried out as he applied more pressure. Her hips danced against his hand as he dipped a finger into her. She was hot, slick, and coated his finger in her delicious wetness.

"That isn't an answer." His lips moved against hers as he placed another kiss on hers, while using his other hand to free himself from his pants. His cock bobbed, ready to dive home.

"No. No panties around you," she cried out.

"Good girl," he muttered. He grabbed her from behind her knees and lifted her up against the door. Holding her still allowed the blunt head of his cock to nestle against her plump lips.

"God, Sid! Stop teasing me!"

His name on her lips was all he needed. The media had gotten to him. They kept mentioning her and the ex, and it was driving him crazy. Slight doubt crept up in the back of his mind about if she was still pining for the other man, but tonight, she had come to him. It was his name on her lips, his cock pushing slowly into her.

He surged forward, causing them both to shout. Her slickness engulfed him, her walls gripping him greedily as he pulled back and pushed forward again.

"Nina," he groaned her name, knowing that he would never tire of her. She gripped his face and crushed her lips to his as she bucked against him, meeting him thrust for thrust.

Their bodies moved in a synchronized motion, bringing pleasure to each of them. He gripped her hips tight as he felt the familiar tingling sensation begin at the base of his balls. He didn't want to come without her. Pulling her away from the door, her legs automatically wrapped around his waist. His pants fell all the way to the floor, allowing him to step out of them.

He took control of their motion and guided her up on his cock and down hard.

She cried out from the new angle. He increased the pace, knowing that his length was going deep. He released a guttural moan from the feel of his cock hitting her womb.

"Faster," she gasped, her breaths coming fast. Her eyes locked on his as he slammed her down onto him again. Her body tightened and she threw her head back, screaming as her release took control of her. He roared as own hit him while he continued to thrust into her, unable to stop as he emptied his seed into her.

She buried her head against his neck as their bodies finally stilled. He tried to catch his breath, but it was coming too fast. His legs shook slightly and he knew he'd better get them to the couch.

"I'm too heavy," she murmured against his neck. "How the hell did we do that?"

He walked toward the couch and lowered her to her feet in front of it. Realizing that she still had her clothes on, he pulled the dress over her head to get rid of it. A snarky comment came to mind, but he didn't want to bring up any of her ex-lovers. Red clouded his vision with the thought of another man between her thighs.

"You have too many clothes on," he muttered, reaching behind her to unsnap her bra.

"Let me kick my shoes off."

"No, they stay on," he growled, pushing her down on the couch.

She barked out a laugh as she laid down before him, spreading her legs wide. The sight of the evidence of their coupling coated her thighs. Some animalistic feeling inside of his chest was pleased to see his release coating her thighs, as if he had just marked her.

He knelt on the couch, mesmerized at the sight before him. His cock began to stiffen again as he reached forward and rubbed his thumb through the wetness and moved up to her labia where more was gathered.

She was perfect and made just for him.

His cock hardened even more.

Her eyes dropped down to his length and widened before meeting his eyes again.

"Come here," she said, opening her arms and legs wider, inviting him to her.

He didn't care what anyone said.

He thrust deep within her, covering her body with his.

She belonged to him.

CHAPTER
eleven

A week later, the media was still in an uproar over Nina and Sid's relationship, but she refused to address anything with them. Rose had been handling them perfectly, but then they upped their attempts to get to her. The media could be like a rabid wolf pack going after a story. Tank had to up the additional security since tons of paparazzi began showing up at her house. Now she couldn't drive herself to the club to meet Sid, so they agreed to move her workouts to her property, being the most secured place. The media would be closed off to her by the closed fence that surrounded her property.

"Go harder," Sid called out as she did her suicide drills. He wanted her to get more cardio in and had set up circuits in the back yard for her. She loved being outside working out. She pushed herself as she ran toward the target and touched the ground before running back to Sid. This was her last run and her legs were burning. They had been outside for a couple of hours, taking advantage of the beautiful weather.

She finally made it to him and slowed down to a walk, her breaths coming fast. Sweat dripped down her face as she tried to catch her breath.

"Good job, babe," he said as she moved to him. He wrapped her up in his arms in a tight hug.

"Ew, I'm sweaty." She laughed, trying to pull back from him.

"I'm not afraid of a little sweat." He gently slapped her round bottom. She knew her ass was one of his favorite features, aside from her breasts. She twisted away from him playfully, swinging her hips as she walked away.

A little sweat? It coated her entire body. Her arms literally glistened from it. He had worked her hard today, but unfortunately, not in a sexual way.

"You've been spending a lot of time in the studio," he noted as he walked alongside of her. She reached down and grabbed her water bottle in passing as they walked, gulping down a healthy swig of the ice-cold water.

"Yeah, I've been working on an independent project." She briefly explained her plan, but left out that the album was a musical documentary of what she went through with Luke, including her meeting him. That part would remain a secret.

Today, she had another producer friend coming into town. The songs she did with Scott were complete, but she wanted to bring in another good friend to include on the project. She was always amazed at how many people would drop whatever they were doing to come and work with her. Of course, she compensated them well for it out of her own money. Since this album would not be on her record label, she had to pick up the cost for everything.

"Sounds awesome," he said as they came to a natural pond on her land. It was one of her favorite spots on her property. She'd had benches built around it so that she could come out and be one with nature.

"I need to fly to L.A.," she informed him as they sat down on a bench.

"Really?"

"Yes. There's an industry award dinner that I've been invited to. I'm nominated for a few awards."

"That's amazing. Good for you." He sat back and laid his arm behind her on the bench. "But why don't you look excited about it?"

She turned to him and smiled. Reaching out, she drew his face closer to hers and they shared a gentle kiss, one that allowed her to draw strength from him. She knew he cared about her. The kiss was so sweet, it brought tears to her eyes.

She was falling fast for Sid. He was too good for her,

and she wanted to protect him from the nasty side of the entertainment business.

"I'm excited," she admitted, pulling back. He laid his forehead against hers and she sighed. "The nominations are from your peers, so it's not just executives making the nominations. It's always humbling to know that people I have worked with have nominated me for my hard work."

"The most recognition I get from Kevin is a six pack of beer once in a while," he chuckled.

She laughed, knowing that Kevin treated him much better than he was admitting.

"Well, I have to go and get fitted for dresses and get to play dress up. That part is fun too. No matter how many events I go to, I love finding the perfect outfit that no one else will have."

He rolled his eyes and she laughed, hitting him with her elbow.

Men!

They never understood women and their clothes. She was no different. Her dressing room was unlike anyone else's in the world. Thank goodness, she had a career where she could afford what she wanted. Clothes and heels were her addiction. A couple times a year, she would go through her clothes and donate her unwanted ones to a women's shelter she secretly financially supported. The women loved it. They didn't know who was donating the clothes, but it gave them a chance to have clothes for job interviews and everyday life.

"When are you leaving?" A glint appeared in his eyes and her breath caught in her throat. She knew that look. It was a fire that burned for her.

"In the morning," she whispered, feeling herself grow slick with need. It didn't matter how many times they'd been together, her body always seemed to react to him.

"Stand up," he instructed. His deep baritone voice caused a shiver to slide down her spine. She placed her bottle down on the ground and did as he asked. Guiding her between his legs, he ran a hand along her leg and up to her hips before taking her ass into his hands. She knew what he was doing.

He was testing to see if she had followed his instructions from last week.

She had.

No panties.

He grunted his pleasure, keeping his eyes on her as he hooked his finger underneath the elastic band of her training shorts before peeling them down. They dropped down to her feet and she kicked them out the way. Her stomach clenched as his eyes moved over her, but she didn't feel the least bit embarrassed in front of him. She should have felt silly for just being in her sports bra and tennis shoes, but she didn't. One look from him and she could feel the moisture seep from between her swollen folds.

She watched him pull his shorts down. She licked her lips at the sight of his long thick cock springing free. She wanted to drop to her knees, but he pulled her to him. She didn't hesitate straddling his waist as he lined up the blunt tip of his cock at her entrance. She held her breath as she pushed down on him, taking him fully within her until she was fully seated on him.

"You're always so wet for me," he groaned as she lifted up and slid back down. Her pussy took him greedily as she moved again, setting the perfect rhythm.

"I like the way you look at me," she replied. She didn't have any other explanation for him, but it was the truth. It was just how her body responded to his. His hands gripped her ass, trying to slow her rhythm down.

"No rush," he ground out. His hands slid up her body to her sports bra and pushed it up to free her bountiful breasts.

"Yes," she hissed as he took one deep into his mouth. She threaded her fingers through his hair as she held him close to her.

She didn't care that they were outside. She owned the property, and if Tank's security was around they would certainly get an eyeful, but she didn't care. She'd hope they would have the decency to give them privacy.

Sid's finger moved down her abdomen and his thumb connected with her swollen clit.

"Are you going to think of me when you're gone?" he asked, nipping her nipple with his teeth. Her pussy walls clenched from the sting of his bite.

"Yes." She rotated her hips, needing him deeper. A warmth spread through her as he worked her clit. The sensations building up in her was getting to be too much as she got closer to her release. She spread her legs farther out on the bench in order to take him deeper, wanting him hit that certain spot that would send her over. "I'm so close, Sid."

"Go ahead, baby. Let go, I've got you," he growled, gripping her ass harder in his hand. His buried hand pinched her clit, finally sending her right to the edge.

His encouragement was all that was needed to send her over the cliff. She let go and her orgasm slammed into her. She cried out, not caring who would be able to hear her as her walls milked his cock. He came as well, shooting his release deep within her.

He held her down on him tight as he came down from his orgasm. She couldn't have moved if someone paid her. She loved the feeling of him nestled deep inside of her. Even semisoft, his cock still gave her a full sensation.

"I think I just gave you a true full workout today," he murmured against her neck.

She barked out a laugh and pulled back to smile at him. Yes, she was falling for him.

"That dress is the one," Meg gushed from her chair. Nina turned around in the three-way mirror as she tried on her custom-made dress. Mallory Divinci was a world-renowned designer who Nina contacted as soon as she decided to attend the event. She immediately set to making Nina a dress for the red carpet for the Writer's Guild Dinner. They had communicated over the past few weeks on a design, and now that Nina had it on, she knew the dress would be worth every penny.

"I'll just have to adjust it. You've lost some weight. Good girl," Mallory noted as she walked around Nina.

"You can have it by tomorrow, right?" Nina inquired. The award show was two days away, but she always demanded the best, and for what she was paying Mallory, it had better be ready.

"Of course, anything for you, Nina." Mallory nodded her head as she began her measurements.

"Hey, Nina!" Tasha motioned to her to get her attention. Turning, she watched as Tasha pulled her phone away from her ear. "Hey, I got a rep from the Writer's Guild on the line. They said that Kenneth Thompson had to pull out of performing and want to know if you could fill in."

Nina glanced at herself in the mirror. This dress was going to kill the red carpet.

"This is short notice," Nina murmured, turning as Mallory had directed.

Tasha replied to whoever was on the phone in a hushed tone.

"He said you'll be the main performance and can do whatever you want."

Nina smirked. They had offered her a performance before, but she was coming off tour and hadn't even planned to go to the event, so she had declined.

Whatever she wanted?

If she performed one of the songs off the upcoming project, that would totally kill the stories of her and Sid. She desperately wanted to get him out of the limelight, as paparazzi had begun to get so bad, she had to have a security team around his condo just to keep them off of him.

Performing a new song would turn the hounds' attention away from Sid and put them on her.

She knew what she had to do.

It wasn't like she didn't like performing, she did, but this would be different.

"I'll do it. Let them know I'll be performing a never

before heard song. They'll have the honor to debut a new single."

Tasha frantically went back to her phone, speaking and negotiating on her behalf.

"What do you want me to do?" Meg asked, instantly bringing out her phone.

Nina knew that pulling a performance together in two days would be crazy, but she would keep it simple.

"Call the band and send the jet. Looks like we'll be performing in two nights."

CHAPTER
twelve

Sid let himself into his house, just as his phone began ringing. He cursed as he tossed his keys on the table behind the couch, shifting his takeout food. He had been waiting for a call from Nina. He hadn't wanted to bother her or seem too overbearing by calling her all the time, so he would wait. He grabbed his phone from his pocket and swiped the screen.

"Hello?"

"Hey, it's me," Nina greeted him. He smiled at the sound of her voice. He walked over to the couch and sat down, placing the food bag on the coffee table.

"Hey yourself. How's L.A.?" he asked, kicking his shoes off and grabbing his remote. He turned the television on to the channel that would be showing the basketball game.

"Eh, L.A. is L.A. I miss home," she murmured in his ear. Just the sound of her voice had his cock thickening. "I miss you."

"I miss you too, babe," he replied back. "What's this I hear about you performing? I thought you weren't on the schedule."

"One of the other performer's father was rushed to the hospital and is deathly ill. So, they called me again to see if I would change my mind about performing."

"Well, that's nice of you," he noted.

Not that he wished anything bad on anyone, but he knew that she was missing the stage. He could tell when she talked about her tours and concerts that she'd performed. His girl was a worldly traveler. The farthest he'd ever been had been to the Bahamas on a guy's trip some years ago. He didn't remember half the trip, having spent most of it drinking.

"I'm performing one of my unreleased songs," she began.

"One from this secret album of yours?" he asked, reaching for his food. He knew the food was bad for him, but he always believed in treating oneself. A good burger was his weakness. Some people's were sweets, but his was a big fat juicy burger. He'd run an extra mile tomorrow to work it off.

He took a bite of his burger and flipped the call to speaker so that he could have both his hands to eat.

"Yes." She paused, and he could tell that something was wrong. He'd been around her long enough to know when something was wrong with her.

"What is it?" he asked. He was never one to bite his tongue.

"The song is about Luke."

He paused chewing and stared at his phone, his mind starting to race. Swallowing his food, he wiped his mouth, not knowing what to say. His appetite had disappeared at the mention of her ex.

Was she rethinking her relationship with the movie star? Was she about to break up with him? They hadn't even labeled their relationship and already he had the sense that she was ending it.

"Look, I really like you and I want to be honest. He hurt me, badly. I don't know any other way to express my feelings than to put pen to pad and sing it out of my system," she admitted with a sigh.

He could sense her hurt and frustration through the phone. If he could, he would go find the man and punch him dead in the face. Then he'd thank him for moving out the way so a real man could have a chance with Nina.

"Do you want to get back with him?" he asked, picking his phone up. He needed to know. If she did, there would be nothing he could do but move aside.

"God, no. I'm only telling you this because I want to be honest with my boyfriend."

Boyfriend?

His heart skipped a beat.

"I'm your boyfriend?" He was grinning like an idiot.

"Well, yeah, silly," she chuckled. "But that was what I didn't tell you. The album is a musical documentary of what I've been going through. It's edgy, hard, and shares my pain. But then I met someone who is brightening my life, someone who is showing me how a man should treat a woman and how relationships should be."

Sid paused and wished desperately that he was with her right now. He'd grab her in his arms and never let her go.

He was falling for her.

Big time.

There was no other reason for why he felt the way he did about her. His daily thoughts were consumed by her. His arms literally ached at the moment to hold her.

"I can't get mad at the way you express yourself. I'm actually proud of you. Do you know how many people don't have an outlet to express their feelings?"

He snagged a fry and felt his appetite coming back with a vengeance. He had missed lunch today, helping Kevin with the plans for the new health club. Since his private client was on the other side of the country, he went with Kevin to meet with the builders who would renovate the building that Kevin had bought.

"You're amazing." He could hear the smile in her voice. "Look, I've gotta go. We're having a rehearsal and they're calling for me."

"Knock em' dead, baby."

"Oh, I plan on it.

"You ready?" Meg asked as the limousine pulled to a halt.

Nina would be lying if she said she wasn't just a tad bit nervous to be walking the red carpet. In the past, she had always walked it with Luke, and this would be the first time she'd be walking a red carpet without him in years.

"As I'll ever be," she murmured, rearranging her dress around her legs. Butterflies filled her stomach as she thought of the dress she was wearing. Thanks to her workouts with Sid, her curves were pronounced, and she knew that she was looking like a million dollars.

The door opened, revealing Tank. He held his hand out and assisted her in getting out of the car. She instantly plastered a smile on her face as the camera flashes lit up the night. She smiled and waved as Tank assisted her a few steps onto the carpet. He would stay a few feet behind her to allow photos to be taken, but if anyone crashed the gate and tried to get to her, they would slam straight into Tank.

"Nina!" Her name was being shouted as she turned

and posed. By the reactions of the crowd, it was the right dress.

Her dress was black, edgy, and showed more skin than she usually did. She had worked her ass off, and she had no problems flaunting her body. The floor length gown was sexy with its one shoulder strap, and she was showing some major leg with the high side-slit that stopped at her groin. Her skinny silver heels completed the ensemble. She had kept her jewelry light, but wanted her makeup to match the edginess of her dress.

Her dark curls flowed down her back. She pulled her hair to one shoulder so that she could show off her new dress as she posed for photos.

"I'll catch up with you!" Meg shouted over the crowd. Nina knew that her sister, as her assistant, would go ahead of her to make sure that the night flowed well.

"Nina, can I get an interview?" a voice called out, causing her to turn toward them. Free Taylor and Ronnie Campbell from the Black News Network were waving to her. She held her clutch in her hand as she walked toward them.

"Hi, guys," she greeted them. They gushed over her gown and new look. She smiled and answered their standard industry questions, such as who was she wearing, was she working on anything new, and questions about her tour. She ended the interview after a few minutes so she could move on.

So many people were shouting her name, vying for her attention. Nina felt bad she couldn't speak to everyone. She made sure she took a few selfies with the fans that lined up by the gates before moving on. She always tried to remember to greet her fans and give them that one-on-one attention.

Tank ushered her over for another quick red-carpet interview. She blew out a deep breath, thankful that she was almost inside.

She walked in front of the wall that housed the names of the sponsors so that she could be photographed by a mob of paparazzi and photographers. She was almost through with the red carpet. Sometimes, this was the hardest part to get through because everyone wanted pictures of her.

"My, my, my..." a familiar baritone voice spoke up behind her.

Not tonight.

She was very familiar with the voice.

She froze and sent up a small prayer, but she knew it was too late. She had almost made it into the facility without running into him.

"Luke."

She turned around and found his eyes devouring her. After all the years they had been together, she knew that look. He wanted her.

Well, he'd lost his right to look at her like that.

She tried to keep her face stoic as she glanced at his side to see his little date holding onto his arm. He moved to her, leaving his date behind. She could hear the chatter from the crowd getting louder. She tried not to roll her eyes because she was sure that this was *the* moment that all the gossip columns were waiting for.

"Wow," he said, arriving in front of her. He took her hand and kissed the back of it while looking into her eyes. She had to fight her first reaction of rubbing his kiss off her skin, but resisted. "You look beautiful."

She didn't need him to tell her that. She'd prefer hearing it from Sid, she chuckled to herself.

As she looked at Luke, she had to admit, he always looked good in his custom tuxedos. His coffee brown skin was flawless, his hair cut low, and he always filled out his suits perfectly.

"You're looking well yourself," she noted, raising her chin higher. She wanted him to look his fill and see what he gave up. He'd lost his chance to have her on his arm at events, and lost the chance to have her in his life.

He. Made. His. Choice.

"Look. We need to talk—"

"I think you said all you had to say to me in Paris," she cut him off. He certainly had expressed his feelings about her and their relationship. After the years they had together, clearly, they didn't mean anything to him. He had ruined their final night in one of her favorite cities in the world. Their night was to be spent celebrating the end of her world tour. Her celebratory spirit was crushed when he decided to end their relationship.

A tight smile came across her face. She knew the public was watching so she'd put on a show. She stared into his eyes and realized that the pain for him wasn't as strong anymore. The reasoning behind their breakup still hurt her. He could have had her love, but he threw it away.

"How long are you in town for? Let me take you out for drinks after the awards tonight." He tried to give her his award-winning smile, but it didn't have any effect on her.

She glanced over his shoulder and found his date standing off to the side with a confused look on her face. She felt pity for the woman. "I don't think that's a good idea."

"Nina—"

"Look, Luke, it was nice seeing you, but I have to go. Take care."

She tried to hold in her smile as she sashayed away from him. She could feel his eyes on her and she smirked.

Too late.

Did she still love him? No, she didn't think so. Deep down, she still cared for him as a human being, but the feeling she thought was love was no longer there. She searched deep within herself, and found her pain was lessening, but her anger was rising. Anger at Luke for hurting her the way he did. Breaking up with her the way he did fueled her emotions for tonight's performance.

Luke would have one hell of a surprise tonight. He wanted to talk? After hearing her song, her name would never cross his lips again.

CHAPTER
thirteen

Sid took a sip of his beer as he sat at the bar. Tonight, he'd invited Kevin out for drinks. They'd went to 4th Street Brewery and it was crowded to capacity.

He wasn't sure why, but he was nervous for Nina. He knew this was what she did for a living, but it didn't stop him from having nerves.

"Y'all getting serious?" Kevin asked, signaling to the bartender for another drink.

"We just put a label to us," Sid announced with a shrug.

"Hot damn." Kevin slapped him on his back with a laugh. Sid tried to keep the smile from spilling out on his face, but he couldn't hold it in.

"I guess it's official. Hell, I didn't even know until she called me her boyfriend," he chuckled, tipping back the rest of his beer.

"Imagine that. Soon you'll be leaving me to go all Hollywood." Kevin sighed, his smile slowly fading.

"You're putting the cart before the horse, man. She's special, and I'm going to take my time. She's not going anywhere, and I'm damn sure not going anywhere." The bartender brought over their food and Kevin's refill.

He glanced up at the television as he bit into his wings, waiting for a sighting of Nina. The bar was buzzing with excitement. Patrons were milling around, chatting about Nina being at the bar. He smirked at the starstruck fans.

"Hey! Be quiet! There she is," a female shrieked, pointing to the television.

A hush fell over the bar while everyone watched Nina step out of the limo.

Sid froze in place as his eyes landed on Nina. His breath escaped his chest as she strode forward, down the red carpet. She was breathtaking.

He could see the confidence in her as she moved. He couldn't take his eyes from her as the women surrounding them were gushing about her gown, her figure, her hair.

"Oh my god. Nina is flawless," a woman sighed.

"I wish I had her body. You heard she's been working with a trainer," another one announced.

"Well, whoever he is, I'd throw my money at him. But isn't she kicking it with her trainer now?"

Kevin nudged him while chuckling at their conversation.

Sid glanced at the women and saw the envy on their faces as they stared at the television with their drinks in hand.

Pride filled his chest as he watched his woman. A little pang of wistfulness resided in his chest. He wished he could be there with her while she had her big moment. She was up for a few awards tonight, and her performance was all the talk.

"I wonder what song she's performing," one of the women murmured.

His thoughts turned to Luke Stow. He didn't know what to expect, but he knew he had to trust her. He wasn't the type of man to play games, and she hadn't given him a reason not to trust her.

"Oh my god! Looks who's behind her!" the women squealed.

His eyes flew up to the television and saw Luke walking up to her. His body grew tense as the television commentators were offering speculations of Nina and Luke's conversation.

"What could he be saying to her?" the man on television asked his co-star.

"He's probably about to beg for her to take him back," the woman snorted.

The shot zoomed in on them. Nina smiled, but Sid knew her. It was fake. He knew she wouldn't want to cause a scene. His eyes took in her body posture and it was stiff. He held back a curse as he watched their inter-action. What he wouldn't give to hear the words that were being exchanged.

"That's a beautiful couple. I hope they're able to work it out," the woman television personality said.

Sid scowled at the woman's comment, and flagged down the bartender for another beer. This was going to be a long night if everyone on television kept talking about the possibility of Nina and Luke getting back together.

The show finally began. Sid and Kevin finished their food and sipped on their beers as they watched. Sid had never been one to watch these types of awards shows, but now he had a reason to.

Two celebrities were on the television to announce the award for Best R&B performance. Sid watched as they flashed different short videos of the artists nomi-nated. His heart skipped a beat when Nina flashed on the screen.

He smiled as the women squealed beside him. Nina would love to know how much her fans were currently rooting for her.

"And the winner is," the actress announced, pausing for a dramatic effect. Sid rolled his eyes, but his breath caught in his throat as he too waited. "Nina Hunt."

The bar went wild as Nina's name was announced.

He laughed, turning to Kevin. They toasted up their beer glasses in celebration.

Someone hushed the bar as Nina finally made her way to the podium. She was all smiles. She glanced around the room as the crowd stood to their feet, giving her a standing ovation. She hugged the award and held a hand to her mouth. He could see through the television that she was holding back tears.

"Wow. You blow my mind." She laughed, looking down at the award again. The crowd quieted to allow her to speak. "I'd first like to thank our heavenly father, for giving me this gift and blessing for me to do what I love every day. I work so hard, and it means so much to me that it has paid off. I'd like to thank everyone at my record label, my team, and the fans. I can't say enough about my fans. And lastly, you know who you are, thank you." She looked into the camera and winked.

His heart slammed in his chest, and he was hit with a realization.

He loved her.

Kevin elbowed him with a laugh as the show went to commercial.

"She's digging you," Kevin joked.

Sid couldn't even keep the silly grin from spreading across his face. He was riding high on cloud nine as the show came back on.

Finally, the moment came—Nina's performance.

The girls next to them were officially tipsy and began chanting for Nina to perform. Before long, the entire bar was chanting Nina's name.

Sid sat forward, not wanting to miss one part of her performance. His heart raced as he waited.

The camera zoomed in on the stage as it went black. It seemed the auditorium, where the show was being held, drew quiet as well.

The lights flashed on, and there was Nina, standing by herself. She had a sexy, black, leather body suit that showed off her legs, with knee-high, black heeled boots. The outfit was tight and highlighted her every curve.

His woman was downright sexy, and his mouth watered just looking at her. Nina Hunt in black leather would be etched into his mind forever.

She would have to wear that same outfit for him one night.

Everything about her was edgy. Her face was fierce as she stared out into the screaming crowd. Somewhere, a fan was blowing on her, causing her hair to flow around her. She was setting the bar of her performance.

The drummer began to play, and the rest of the band joined in a few seconds later. She did a sexy dance move that drove not only the crowd on television crazy, but the people around him wild.

He was captivated by her.

No wonder people loved her. She belonged on that

stage. It was like looking at a different person. She had a different persona on the stage, and was no longer the shy Nina that he had gotten to know.

No, this was the superstar Nina Hunt.

And she owned it.

She began to strut toward the crowd, and like magic, two dancers appeared at her sides. They did a short dance routine before she brought the microphone to her lips.

Do you see tears in my eyes?
You didn't love me the way you said you did.
Watch my fat ass move past you.
You're no good for me.
I don't need you or your money.
I got enough of my own.
But don't worry, I still know how to smile.
I still got it. Bringing all the men in.
You've lost a good one.

He smiled as she worked the crowd. She had them eating out the palm of her hand. He and Kevin laughed every time the camera zoomed in on Luke's face for a reaction. The actor tried to keep his face emotionless, but Sid could see the regret.

Nina's song was just as she said it would be— edgy, and filled with anger and pain. She was laying her emotions on the table for all the world to see. Strobe lights flew across the stage to add to the edginess of the performance.

Her guitarist came up to her and played next to her. He could see that they knew each other well, the way they played off of each other.

I can smile, I'm good on my own.

You're my motivator.

I can smile, I'm good on my own.

You're my motivator.

The camera would zoom in on her as she strolled over with her dancers to the part of the stage where Luke was seated in the front row with his date.

Sid leaned forward.

She wouldn't.

She sang the hook again, but this time in front of her ex, and flipped him the bird.

The crowd went wild.

Nina put her feet up as she sat back in her recliner on her private jet. Her band was still riding high on the performance and opted to stay in L.A. a little longer. They deserved to party. She put them up in a hotel, all expenses paid by her so that they could party the weekend away.

Partying all weekend wasn't her style. She was homesick for Cleveland. She had someone to rush home to, so she flew out after the performance.

She glanced over at Meg and found her asleep in her recliner. She felt the signs of sleep coming for her too, so she stood from her chair and made her way back to her private bedroom. They had only been in the air for about a half an hour and were in for a quiet trip.

Four more hours to go.

By the time they got to Cleveland, it would be early morning. She hadn't wanted to wait, and preferred to fly at night since it was always quiet at the airport when they arrived. Paparazzi and fans wouldn't know when to expect her should they be waiting for her when she arrived.

She kicked off her shoes, leaving her yoga pants and T-shirt on and dove into the bed. Turning on the television, she snuggled down into the plush blankets. She flicked through the channels until she found a show that was replaying her performance.

"This is her official response to Luke leaving her. Why shouldn't she be mad?" The woman threw up her hands. "She's the biggest female music star right now in the world. She can say and do whatever she wants!"

They were doing a play-by-play of her performance as if they were discussing sports. Nina chuckled, thinking that the media always wanted to try to read more into what was there, but for once they got it right. She was pissed when she wrote that song. All the emotions from the night in Paris came to the forefront as she performed in front of Luke.

"Look at her face, it is fierce. She's not playing. This was a woman who wanted her ex to see that he didn't break her." The other woman agreed.

Nina giggled at the memory of her flipping him off. She couldn't believe she had actually done it, and his reaction was priceless. She could remember how his eyes narrowed on her as he sat back in his chair. His poor date seemed embarrassed by the spectacle because, of course, the entire world would be paying attention to Luke and Nina.

The room had gone crazy. Almost every person in the room had been on their feet as she performed.

She got exactly what she'd wanted. The media was now in a frenzy around her and Luke again. They would leave Sid alone and let him live in peace. She buried down further in the covers as the two women on the television began to talk about her weight loss. She frowned at it, but realized it didn't matter.

All that mattered was getting home to a certain some-one. *Someone worth writing a love song about*, she thought as she drifted off to sleep.

CHAPTER
fourteen

Sid bit back a yawn as he got ready to leave for a run. It was a little after nine in the morning, and he was off today. He didn't know when Nina would be returning to Cleveland, since he hadn't heard from her. He grabbed his cell phone from the back of his couch and checked to see if he had missed any calls.

Nothing.

He figured a celebrity like her would have been out last night at one of the crazy parties they were talking about on TV last night, but knew that wasn't his Nina. If she did, she would have been the one in the corner, celebrating with close friends.

He didn't want to be overbearing and call her, so he figured he'd wait on her. He trusted her. After watching that performance, he didn't have any doubt where her mind was.

She was done with Luke Stow.

The doorbell rang, catching his attention. He walked over, swung it open and froze in place.

"Nina," he breathed. She stood there, wearing a white flower print dress that stopped at her knees and high-heeled wedges. Her face was covered by large glasses as she stood there, returning his stare.

A smile spread across her face as she flew into his arms. He slammed the door closed as his lips automatically crashed onto hers.

She had come home to him.

He bent down and lifted her up high in his arms as he began moving toward the stairs.

"When did you get into town?" he asked against her lips as he took the stairs, still carrying her. He refused to let her go until he could deposit her onto his bed.

"About two hours ago." She trailed kisses along his face and down to his neck. He growled when she nipped the skin of his neck with her teeth. His hand slid underneath her dress as he walked into his bedroom.

She was bare beneath her dress.

"You drive me crazy," he admitted, tossing her down onto the bed.

"Same here," she teased as she pulled her dress back up, revealing a very naked Nina. His cock pushed painfully against his shorts as he stared down at her bare pussy.

He hooked her by her legs and pulled her to the edge of the bed as he kneeled by it. He missed having the taste of her on his tongue. He spread her legs and began to feast on her naked flesh.

She cried out when his tongue slid between her labia. As always, she was wet for him. His tongue dove deeper as he spread her legs wider.

"Sid," she groaned, her fingers gripping his hair as she began to ride his tongue. He couldn't get enough of her. He made sure to pay close attention to her little bud of nerves.

He slid two fingers deep within her as he focused his attention on her clitoris, alternating between sucking on it and flicking it with his tongue. Her hips thrust against his fingers as she rode his hand and his mouth.

Her body shook as he devoured her. He loved hearing his name on her lips as she called out his name again. Her sweetness poured out of her, coating his fingers as he continued to thrust them deep inside of her tight channel. He nipped at her clit, sending her over the edge. The muscles in her legs tightened on against his head but he pushed them apart, not wanting to stop. She released a scream as her orgasm gripped her. Sid drank in every bit of her release as it coated his tongue.

Her body slowly relaxed on the bed, and he had to laugh. He pulled his fingers from her, licking them clean.

Standing, he snatched his shirt off and got rid of the rest of his clothes, not taking his eyes off of her.

His heart was racing as he realized that she'd left L.A. immediately and came straight to him.

Her eyes opened and locked on his. She sat forward on the bed, eye level with his cock that was bobbing for her attention. She gripped it with her hand as she stared into his eyes. Her small hand began to stroke his long length before gliding it into her mouth. He hissed as he watched the tip disappear deep into her mouth.

It wasn't until he hit the back of her throat that he remembered to breathe. She pulled back and scooted closer toward him as he gently gripped her head.

"Open your mouth wider," he urged, trying to hold back. He wanted to shove it deeper into her mouth, but he didn't want to hurt her. He ached to feel her slick pussy surrounding his cock, but her mouth was just as delicious.

She groaned, her eyes closing as he began to gently thrust in and out her mouth. The sensation of her tongue swirling on the underside of his cock drove him crazy. He bit his lip to keep from shouting.

"Yes, Nina. Keep doing what you're doing," he growled. He could feel the quickening sensation deep within his balls. He was close and didn't want to shoot off in her mouth. He wanted to feel her wrapped around him. As the sensation built, he squeezed his eyes shut, trying to fight his orgasm. He wasn't quite ready yet. He wanted this to last longer.

"Baby, you're going to have to stop," he announced, pulling his cock from her mouth and her reach. He pushed her down and covered her body with his. Her legs immediately spread for him.

"I missed you so much," she panted as she pulled his head down to hers. Their lips met in a searing kiss. His tongue pushed forward, sweeping her mouth so that he could taste her.

His cock brushed against her slick folds, and with one thrust, he slid inside. He broke the kiss and gasped as her hot heat gripped him. Her legs wrapped around his waist, holding him in place.

She threw her head back, displaying her soft, creamy brown skin that he loved to run his tongue along. His lips moved to taste her skin as he thrust hard into her. "Please, don't stop."

"Nina." He growled against her neck as her moans and gasps fueled his desire for her. His hips quickened their pace as she her legs gripped his waist tighter. "You belong to me."

"Yes!" Her nails dug into his shoulders as he thrust harder, needing to get closer to her.

"Say it," he growled. An animalistic need to hear her say the words burst forth in his chest.

Her eyes opened and met his. Need filled her eyes, and he could feel the muscles in her body growing tight.

"I belong to you," she screamed as another orgasm came over her. He gripped her tight to him as he roared his release, spilling his seed into her.

Nina rested her head against Sid's solid chest. She trailed her fingers along his flat brown nipple. His breaths were even and slow as he slept. Flying overnight was well worth it.

Her body was relaxed and satisfied from the entire day being spent in bed. If this was what she would come home to from a long road trip, she'd have to go away again just so that Sid could ravage her body in the same fashion as today.

"You keep that up and you'll be getting something started again," he murmured, his hand coming up to rest on hers.

She giggled as she shifted her naked body next to his. Her breasts were pushed against his side.

"Well, considering how long we've been in here, someone may have reported us missing," she joked.

"Let them look for us," he murmured, turning toward her and bringing her closer to him. She tilted her head back and smiled. His semihard length pressed against her stomach as she tried to concentrate on his face, but her attention was slowly being drawn to his stiffening member.

"They would certainly find something." She grinned, her hand making its way down his abdomen.

"Nope," he chuckled, grabbing her hand. "I need to feed you. As much as I want to continue feasting on your delicious body, we do need to eat."

"Okay." She pouted. "What do you have in mind?"

"Let me take you out for an early dinner," he suggested, looking past her shoulder. She turned around and saw that it was after five in the afternoon.

"Wow. Time sure flies when you're having fun," she giggled. Sitting up in the bed, the sheet slid off her.

"As much as I'm loving this sight, we've got to eat," he chuckled as he reached out and tweaked her beaded nipple. Her stomach grumbled, announcing itself. A giggle escaped her lips as she tucked her hair behind her ear. She leaned down and laid a kiss on the corner of his mouth.

"Feed me, Sid," she whispered seductively. His hand reached up and cupped her cheek, his thumb brushing her cheek as he stared into her eyes. His lips turned up in a crooked smile as he gazed into her eyes.

"I'm falling for you," he blurted out, his blue eyes searching hers.

Her breath caught in her throat. She could feel her eyes burning as she fought back tears.

"I think I'm falling for you too." She smiled.

Her stomach growled again, and this time it was so loud, the neighbors probably heard it. They both burst out laughing.

"Come on, before your stomach jumps out and goes scavenging for food on its own." Sid smiled as he got out of bed and headed into the bathroom.

The sound of music floating through the air caught her attention.

Her cell phone.

She grabbed it off the nightstand and froze at the name flashing across the screen.

Luke Stow.

She cursed and let it go to her voicemail. She placed it down on the nightstand and moved to go into the bathroom, but it began to ring again. She snatched it up.

Luke Stow.

"Hello," she huffed.

"Nina, it's me," Luke announced.

"What do you want?" She wasn't going to beat around the bush with him. She didn't know why he could be calling her.

"Look, I—" He stopped and blew out a deep breath. "First, I want to apologize to you."

She paused, not believing the words that were coming out of his mouth.

"Why are you doing this?" she asked, pushing her hair behind her hair.

"Because your performance hit me in the chest."

She rolled her eyes and stood from the bed. She couldn't find anything to cover herself so she pulled the sheet from the bed and wrapped it around her. Walking to the window, she pushed the curtain aside and her eyes landed on the security guard she had hired to keep the media away from Sid. The street was quiet once again.

"Well, it was more about me needing to get shit off my chest than for you."

"I know, and it made me realize how much I hurt you. I never meant to do that. You know I'm getting pressure from the studio—"

"You will not blame the studio for you breaking up with me," she snapped. She moved from the window and began to pace the room. How dare he try to tell her that it was the studio that made him break up with her.

"You've never understood what I go through. They said I had an image to uphold and they didn't think us being together was helping."

"Are you kidding me? So you put your career ahead of me and our relationship? You made your decision," she argued.

"Baby, please. Give me another chance. I know now what I did was wrong. I miss you."

"You don't get to call me that. You lost that right," she hissed. Anger filled her chest that he thought he could just call her, apologize, and that she would go running back to him.

"What do you want me to do? Beg?" he countered. "If that's what I have to do, then I'll do it. Nina, give me another chance. You know we're good together."

Well, he should have thought about that before letting Hollywood executives dictate his life. It wasn't like she was just any common woman. She was Nina Hunt. But all of that didn't matter anymore.

She closed her eyes and counted to ten, regretting answering her phone. She should have let it go to voicemail and followed Sid into the bathroom.

"Everything okay in here?" Sid asked, coming out of the bathroom.

"Who the hell is that?" Luke snapped.

"None of your business," she taunted. Her eyes locked on Sid walking toward her with nothing but a towel tucked around his waist.

"Who is that?" Sid asked, his eyes narrowed on her phone.

"You're with that white boy, aren't you? It's true. You're dating your trainer," Luke scoffed.

"It's none of your business, Luke," she snapped. She

heard Sid's quick intake of breath at the mention of her ex's name.

"Look, we all make our mistakes. Just forgive me and I'll forgive you for the white guy, baby. Come back to me and I'll make you forget that all of this ever happened," Luke promised.

If she could reach through the phone and choke him, she would.

"Goodbye, Luke."

CHAPTER
fifteen

Silence filled the air in the car as Sid drove them to a local restaurant. Nina sat in the passenger seat, barely talking to him. He wasn't sure what the ass had said to her, but he could see that it shook her up. The guard that was assigned to him followed them in the car behind them. He had argued with Nina that he didn't need a guard.

Now that most of the media and paparazzi had left his street, he didn't need it. He only agreed to it because of the disruption of the traffic and street due to the media. It was more so for the protection of his neighbors than him.

He didn't like the silence. They'd had an enjoyable day spent in the bed, making love for hours. Now it had been ruined by a telephone call from her ex. But he knew that it was more than just talking to her ex. Something was said that made her withdraw. He had practically admitted to loving her, and now they were traveling in complete silence.

He pulled into the parking lot of the restaurant and shut off the car.

"Spit it out," he huffed as he turned to her. He needed her to spill whatever was bothering her. She glanced at him, but she had her large glasses on her face, so he reached over and removed them.

Her eyes were red from crying.

"Nina, please tell me what it is," he urged, not liking to see her like this.

"When you look at us together, what do you see?" she asked softly.

Anger began to grow in his chest, realizing that fucker had played the race card on her, trying to make her feel guilty for dating out of her race. He grabbed her hand and brought it to his lips, laying a gentle kiss to the back of her hand.

"When I look at you, I see the most beautiful woman in the world. A woman that takes my breath away. Someone I absolutely love making love to," he murmured against the back of her hand.

She smiled a sad smile as he reached up and brushed away a tear that escaped her eyes.

"You're just saying that," she murmured.

He shook his head. If ever he and Luke Stow were to meet in person, he would have to straighten him out.

Luke should not have brought his name up at all. If he had a problem with him being with Nina, he could come talk to him man to man. Sid brushed her hair from her face as he stared at her.

"I see the most gorgeous brown skin that makes me want to explore it. I've been fascinated with how soft it is, and the taste of it." He trailed a hand down her cheek to her lips, his eyes following suit. "These plump lips call to me. They scream for me to touch them with mine, to taste you, and every time I do, I swear you get sweeter."

Her eyes grew wider as she leaned toward him.

"I love the look of your dark areolas and the moles that are scattered around your breasts. When I bury my face between your brown thighs, I love how you spread yourself open before me."

She sighed as their foreheads met. He could hear her breaths coming fast as she listened to his words. He was painfully aroused just thinking of her beautiful body being laid out before him, ready for him to take her.

"Sid," she whispered.

"So you asked me what I saw when I looked at you. I see you—all of you."

"I'm wet just thinking of your words," she whispered with a smile.

There she was.

His Nina.

"Baby, your body was made for me. I don't think I've

ever found you not ready for me," he chuckled, pleased that he was able to bring her out of her funk. He pressed a small kiss to her mouth.

"I'm starving. Have you been here before?" she asked, pulling back. She snatched her glasses from his lap and put them back on her face.

"Their food is amazing. Let's go, superstar. Let me feed you."

Nina had finally chosen a date to drop her independent album that she named after herself.

Nina.

The album was one of her most personal albums to date. Never had she ever went so deep and shared so much of herself with the world.

Time flew by quickly as they finished the album. She had one more song to record that she had written. She had been bringing in other producers that would help her with the album who she knew shared her vision.

"What's this last song you want to record?" Vin asked, swiveling his chair toward her. Vin Forbes was one of the biggest music producers in history. He had worked with all the greats before her. They had worked on previous records before, and she knew she couldn't do an independent album without him.

"A love song." She smiled, looking up from her tablet. While recording the album, she didn't have too many people in the studio as she normally did. A few of the songs she allowed others to come in, but today was not one of those days.

The last song on the album had to be perfect. The songs were a range of her life from anger to sorrow, to acceptance and peace, and to love. It was a direct reflection of her life since Luke had broken up with her. Once this album was out, it would help her close a certain chapter of her life and allow her to move on.

He smiled at her, and she could see that genius brain of his working. He sat there staring at her while he rubbed his chest-length beard. She always laughed at Vin's man bun. Some men couldn't pull it off, yet he did in a rugged mix of country and hip hop.

"What?" she chuckled as she unfolded her legs from beneath her.

"Is it about this new boyfriend of yours?"

"It might be." She smiled, thinking of Sid. Her heart wanted to sing when she thought of his smiling face, or the faces he made when he was climaxing during their lovemaking.

"Somebody's in love," he teased.

She couldn't stop the silly grin from spreading across her face. Just thinking of Sid either had her smiling like an idiot, or getting painfully aroused and ready to jump his body.

"Leave me be," she chuckled, rolling her eyes.

"For now, we have to work. I have plenty of time to tease my favorite singer about her falling in love. Jump on the keyboards and let me hear what you're thinking about," he instructed.

He was just as easy to work with as Scott. They worked so well together, she knew he would understand where she was coming from. They complimented each other well musically, and that was why she wanted a one-on-one with him before they brought in the engineers.

Sitting down at the keyboard, she began playing a few cords to give him an idea of what she wanted.

"Okay." He bowed his head, listening as she continued to play.

She knew the words to the song already and couldn't help herself from singing the words of the ballad.

When I close my eyes, I feel you near me.
You make me feel safe and loved.
No one has made me feel this way before.
When I close my eyes, I feel your love.
You made me realize what love is.
No one had ever loved me the way you do.

"That's hot. Keep going." He grabbed his guitar, and a second later, he joined her. The air filled with the sweet melody of his guitar as it joined the sounds of the piano.

I'll always love you.

Whether we say the words or not.

I'll always love you.

No matter what the world thinks.

I'll always love you.

They continued playing together until they were able to get the music down just right before she went into the booth. She knew that once she brought the band in and add all the instruments, it would be an amazing song.

This song had to be perfect. It was her love song to Sid. It only seemed right that the first song on the album represent her anger and pain, and the last song to show that she had found true love.

They worked together for hours before Meg burst through the door, just as Nina was coming out of the booth.

Her phone vibrated, and she could see that it was Luke calling. She rolled her eyes and sent the call to voicemail. She didn't have time for his crap. She stuffed her phone in her back pocket, having already ignored countless amounts of calls from him.

"Hey, sis," she greeted with a hug.

"How's it going in here?" she asked as she flopped down on the couch.

"Your sister is a musical genius," Vin bragged, typing out a few commands on his laptop.

"The people I work with just make me look good." She laughed. "This is the last song, and I believe *Nina* is complete.

"So that's the title? Your first name?"

"Yup." Nina came and sat next to her sister. "The album shares pieces of me with the world."

"Cool. I was coming to let you know that we're making final arrangements for the release now that you've picked a date. We have tons to get done. The photoshoot is coming up. I've made those arrangements and we need to get you ready."

Nina sighed, knowing what she was about to be up against. It wouldn't end with just the photoshoot, there were plenty of small things that were coming up as part of her releasing an album without the backing of her label. So the brunt of the work was falling on her team, who had been working tirelessly around the clock while she'd been putting the final touches on her album.

"This album is fire. It's like Nina has an alter ego," Vin chuckled. "I can't wait for the album release party. Everyone is going to love it."

"Where does Damien want to do the photoshoot?" Nina asked, feeling her phone vibrate in her back pocket. She pulled it out and glanced down at the screen.

Luke.

"Are you kidding me? He's calling you?" Meg asked, looking down at her phone.

"Yeah. He won't stop," she murmured, sending the call to voicemail.

"What could he possibly want?" she asked, flabbergasted.

"Believe it or not, he wants me to take him back."

"Fuck. Are you thinking about it?"

"What? God, no." Nina shook her head.

The relationship with Sid was going well. He was all that she could think about. The feelings she had had for Luke were just about a distant memory. Sid had helped her see that what she had with Luke wasn't love. She knew what she shared with Sid was the real thing. They had yet to say the words, but she knew he loved her. She could tell by every kiss they shared, every flicker of his tongue on her body as he worshipped her, that he loved her.

They weren't rushing into anything.

For what?

If love between them was meant to be, it would be meant to be.

Damn the difference in skin color. Nina always believed that a person loved who they loved.

It still bothered her that when the media spoke of Sid, they always had to call him her *white* boyfriend, or her the *white guy* she's dating. Why couldn't it just be her boyfriend or the man she was currently seeing?

"Anyhoo, where are we going for the photoshoot?" she asked again, shaking her head to clear her thoughts.

"Atlanta."

CHAPTER
~sixteen~

Nina's sweat-soaked body fell across Sid's chest. He tried to catch his breath but it was coming too fast. Her walls continued to milk his cock as he stayed nestled within her slick cocoon. He reached up and brushed her hair from her face, trying to get a peek at her.

He would never get enough of her.

Her eyelashes cast shadows on her cheeks as she laid on top of him, breathing just as fast as he was.

"You all right?" he murmured, shifting her to his side. She gave a weak protest as he withdrew from her body.

"Hmm..." was her reply as she shifted onto her bed. He slowly crept from the bed, walked into her en suite and snagged a washcloth. Running it under the warm water, he wiped himself down and glanced at himself in the mirror, smirking as he saw the evidence of their love-making. Nina was a little sex kitten in the bed. She always left her mark on him.

He walked back to the bed and climbed back in it.

He gently moved her legs apart so that he could clean her. A quick intake of breath from her made him look up at her to find her eyes on him.

"You always take such good care of me," she whispered as he continued to wipe the evidence of their release from between her legs.

He smiled as he finished and tossed the cloth to the floor, climbing back in beside her. The lamp from the nightstand was the only light in the room, casting a soft glow around them. He pulled her close and snagged the plush blankets to cover them. She nestled into his side, resting her head in the crook of his arm.

"It pleases me to take care of you. There are only so many ways that I can spoil you," he murmured, brushing her hair from her face. He stared down at her and knew that whatever she asked of him, he would do.

He may not be able to spoil her in the monetary fashion, but he would give her anything her body, heart, and soul desired.

"I have to travel for a photoshoot, and I was wanting to ask you to come with me," she said, searching his eyes.

Nina almost seemed nervous about whatever she was about to say, so he chuckled as he gathered her close to him. The feel of her plump breasts crushed to his chest, causing his cock to harden once more. He ran a hand down her back and to the swell of her ass. He couldn't keep his hands off of her.

"You want me with you?" he growled playfully.

"I do," she giggled. He loved the sound of her laugh. Sid could see that being a recording artist was not all fun and games. It was very stressful on her. She had to please so many fans and had tons of people who depended on her to feed their families.

"And what's your reasoning for wanting me with you?" His hand tightened on the firm meat of her ass as her hand traveled down his abdomen. She trailed her fingers along the ridges of his muscles.

"Well, I certainly can't keep leaving this behind." She grasped his cock in her hand. "This is a treasure. I can't risk having some other woman discovering it."

He closed his eyes and bit back a moan as she continued to stroke him.

"You don't have to worry about any other woman," he proclaimed. Cheating was not in his nature. Never had he ever cheated on a woman. He wasn't one to play those types of games. If he felt it was time to go their separate ways, he just cut it off.

"I know, but like I said, this isn't something I should just leave lying around," she joked as she circled the head of his cock. He squeezed her hard in his hand as she slid down to the base of his length and cupped his balls in her hands. "I need to make sure it's getting plenty of work."

He growled deep in his throat as he rolled over on

top of her. She laughed as he settled between her thighs, positioning the blunt tip of his cock at her entrance.

"You want to take me on as your personal sex toy?" He thrust deep into her slick core and paused at the familiar feeling of her walls gripping him. He would never grow old of this. He could stay buried within the depths of her pussy forever.

"Yes. I want to have full access to you too." He laughed, thinking of the request he had made of her. She had yet to let him down. Any outfit that she wore for him —dress, pants or shorts—she was always bare for him. He enjoyed being able to access her pussy whenever the desire struck him, and not having to fight with a scrap of panties.

"Is that right?" He moved her arms above her head and entwined their hands together. He sat back on his heels, still deep within her. He loved the sight of her spread out on the bed just for him. The contrast of their skin against each other was a complete turn on. He loved the warm bronze color of her skin next to his lighter skin tone.

This was his woman.

He loved everything about her.

He pulled back and thrust slowly.

Images of her round and ripe with his child sucker punched him in his chest.

He knew without a doubt that he loved her.

His hips quickened with the thought of them having a future together, of her bearing their children, raising those children and growing old together.

That fantasy of her belly swollen with his child fueled his desire for her. He knew that any children they had would be beautiful. Hopefully, they would take after their mother. He grabbed her hips to change his angle to get deeper.

"Sid!" she shouted as he lost control of himself. He braced himself over her, her hands finding their way into his hair, locking on the strands as he claimed her in his own way. She cried out as her body shook from her release.

"Nina!" He yelled her name as he poured himself into her.

Damien Jones was one the most sought-after photographers in the world. Nina had reached out to him to do the official shoot for her album because she knew he would be able to get the grittiness she was looking for, and could flip the scene to soft to reflect the lighter side of the record.

Two hours of hair and makeup, and Nina was seconds from going on strike.

"Are we done yet?" she snapped, irritated that it was taking so long.

"Calm down, we're done," Sebastian, her makeup artist, huffed. If she didn't say anything he would take forever and a day. He was a perfectionist, and a damn good one too. "I'm working with a masterpiece and you know that takes time."

"Ha-ha," Nina grumbled as he moved away from her. Wardrobe flew around her instantly as she stood from his chair.

"Be careful of her makeup!" Sebastian snapped as they led her away.

"You heard the man. He'll fight someone if my makeup gets messed up," she chuckled as she was helped into her leather body suit. It molded perfectly to her body, displaying all the curves that she had worked so hard for. She glanced in the mirror and was satisfied with her choice of outfit.

Finally finished with her outfit, Sebastian gave her one more look and gave his approval. She was finally ready to go onto the set. Damien had chosen an outdoor set on top of a building.

Sid had come with her. She knew that he would be with Meg, who would be giving him the rundown of the day. They had been at the site for almost four hours and had yet to take a single picture.

Wardrobe, makeup, and hair followed her out to the

set. They would pluck, tease, and ensure that she was flawless for the photographer.

"Damien." She smiled as she stepped out onto the roof. The sky and lighting was perfect. The building itself was exactly what she was looking for, and she knew that this was going to be an amazing shoot.

"Nina, darling." Damien opened his arms to her and gently hugged her, giving two air kisses on each side of her face. "You look beautiful. You ready?"

"Thanks. Let's do this." She looked over to where Sid and Meg sat in their chairs. Giving him a wink, she saw his eyes narrowed on her. She could see from where he sat that he approved of her outfit. The slow trail of his eyes over her body before they met hers again, had her clenching her thighs together.

He winked back at her.

Damien guided her over to where he wanted to start. She had to pay attention to him, as he would be directing her throughout the shoot.

"I want you to think of the song that you performed. Girl, that song was fierce," Damien encouraged, wanting her to dig down for the emotions he wanted for the shot. She thought back to the night of the awards ceremony and felt the anger rising. "Perfect."

She followed his directions as he led her. Look right. Bend down. Hold the hair up. Turn around. Look off into the distance.

The commands kept coming, and finally, she was able to take a break. Sebastian and the hair stylist, Leah, swooped down on her to touch up her hair and makeup. They both fussed over her as she was whisked away, back to wardrobe, for the second outfit and the next part of the shoot.

She returned in a gown that flowed around her thighs. It was white and hung off both shoulders. Her jewelry and heels were gold. Leah had added extensions to her hair earlier, and this time, her hair flowed down her back in waves. Before going back for the second round of photos, she hurried over to where Sid stood. He was chatting with one of the light guys as she made her way over to him.

"Hey, you. Making friends?" she joked as she walked into his open arms. The guy got called away and left them alone.

"You can say that," he murmured, turning his attention to her. "You're absolutely gorgeous."

He lowered his head to hers. Even with her heels, she had to stretch to meet him for a hot, searing kiss. Feeling his hand disappear beneath her dress, she knew that he would find her thong. She didn't want to chance the wind gusting up and causing her dress to fly up, giving everyone a show.

"You mess up my makeup, and you might have to deal with Sebastian," she chuckled, pulling back. Sid looked over her shoulder at the very flamboyant makeup artist.

"I think I can take him." Sid smiled down at her. "But I see someone was a bad girl."

She smiled at him while she whispered her reasoning. "I just didn't want to show off the goods if a good wind came through here."

"I'll just have to think of a creative punishment for you," he chuckled. Her core clenched with the thought.

Her name was called and she glanced over her shoulder, seeing that they were ready for her.

"Well, duty calls," she said, standing on her tiptoes to give him one last kiss. "Later, we can go out to one of my favorite spots here in Atlanta. Just me and you."

"It's a date."

CHAPTER
~seventeen~

"I don't dance," Sid announced as the car pulled to a halt in front of one of the popular night lounges in the heart of Buckhead, Georgia.

"Don't worry. They have a nice lounge and VIP section where we can chill, eat, and just listen to music," Nina replied with a small smile.

Tank opened Sid's door and he stepped out. Walking around the car, Sid opened Nina's door and offered her his hand. As she stepped out of the car, people in line for the lounge began recognizing her. She had changed into a bright pink dress that looked like a button-down shirt with a wide brown belt that cinched in at her waist to show off her new hourglass figure. He loved that the dress stopped mid-thigh, and how it showed off her toned legs. Her heels made him want to throw her over his shoulder and take her back to the hotel.

"Nina!" The crowd grew frantic at the knowledge that she was going into the establishment that they were waiting to get into. Fans called out to her, begging for her to stop and talk with them.

"This way." Tank motioned for them to follow him. In this situation, Tank had extra guards tonight to keep Nina safe.

Sid entwined his fingers with Nina's as they followed Tank. Nina waved to the fans calling for her to come take pictures with them. She didn't ask to stop, so he ushered her right into the building amid the flash of people trying to snap pictures of her. The lounge held an upscale ambiance to it that allowed Sid to relax. Nina had good taste in venues, and it looked like they would be able to have a great time.

Nina's body pressed close to him as they made their way through the establishment. Tank led them up to the VIP section that gave them a bird's-eye view of the dance floor. A U-shaped leather booth with a table allowed for eating.

He assisted Nina into the booth before sliding in beside her.

"I promise, you'll love the food here," she said, leaning toward him so that he could hear her. The music was loud, and the bass sent vibrations through their booth.

The waitress came over and introduced herself, then took their drink orders and left them the food menus.

"What would you suggest?" He pulled her closer to his side so that they could hear each other.

"The lamb chops are out of this world," she said close to his ear. She pointed on the menu, but his thoughts weren't on food.

This trip opened his eyes to the real Nina. Even though she was this megastar, she was still the same person when she interacted with him, her team, and even the fans. She was just Nina. He stretched his arm along the back of the booth and looked out into the crowd. Tank stood off near the entrance to their section to keep the fans at bay. Most glanced over and kept going, as everyone was out having a good time. It was a good mix of a crowd. The music switching from rap, to R&B, to electric. The DJ was playing music to appeal to everyone in the crowd.

"I like coming to the clubs and lounges to get a feel of what people are in to," she said, leaning into him.

"That's a smart idea," he replied, leaning down to her ear where she could hear him. It made sense to him. She didn't have to pay for surveys or test groups or anything. She could just go straight to the source.

A club.

The waitress brought their drink orders and took their food orders.

He leaned back against the booth and took a sip of his drink. A song came on that everyone in the lounge knew and they flew to the dance floor, or stood where they were, and began singing along with the song. It was a female singing a racy, fast song.

"Recognize the vocals?" She smiled at him with her glass in her hand.

"That's you?" he asked. He wasn't familiar with the song, but apparently, everyone else was.

She nodded while swaying back and forth to the beat. His eyes took in the entire place, and every single person either sung along with the song or danced to it. She had a God-given talent that was not being wasted.

The song went off and was replaced by a slow ballad with a husky woman's voice singing about missing her lover.

He leaned over to her, letting his lips brush against her earlobe. "Do you have those panties on?"

Her eyes shot to his as she played with the straw in her glass. She didn't say a word, but nodded her head.

"Take them off," he commanded. He leaned back and found her eyes wide. He didn't think she would take the bait since they were in a public place, with the occasional person looking over at them.

He kept his eyes on hers as she placed her glass on the table. She looked around first before shimmying out of the panties. She handed them to him.

"You happy?" She cocked her eyebrow at him. He

took the small scrap of material from her and shoved it deep within his pocket.

He shook his head.

Her eyes grew wide as she returned his stare.

"You're not?" Her voice ended on a cute squeak. He pulled her back to him and leaned down to her.

"Not by a long shot," he whispered. His hand disappeared beneath the table as his eyes locked on hers.

No words escaped from her mouth as his hand slipped beneath the protective barrier of the table. He slid his fingers along her thigh.

"You wouldn't." Her eyes began taking in the crowd, checking to see if anyone was looking at them.

He didn't care if they were. His attention was captured by the beauty in the pink dress next to him. She knew he only had one request of her and she finally slipped up.

"Is that a dare?" he asked, cocking an eyebrow at her. He was very competitive in nature, and rarely backed down for challenges or dares.

Even in the darkened area, he could see her nipples push against her dress. His little kitten was getting aroused with the thought of a little play in public. The edges of his lips rose in a smile.

That's why he loved her.

His hand glided up her thigh as her legs parted for him. He leaned his forehead against hers, knowing that if anyone were to look their way, would think that they were just sharing an intimate moment, but not realizing how intimate it truly was.

His fingers dove between her folds and found her little nub already slick with her arousal.

Every. Single. Time.

She was already wet for him, which drove his cock wild. It pushed painfully against his jeans as his finger became coated in her sweetness.

He moved his head so that he could speak in her ear.

"You never fail to amaze me. This goes to show that this pussy belongs to me," he whispered.

She bit her lip as he flicked her swollen flesh.

"Don't close your eyes," he murmured. He wanted her to look around at all the people in the room as he brought her to orgasm.

"They're going to see us," she gasped. He dipped his fingers farther, gathering more of her moisture and bringing it back to her clit. She automatically spread her legs even wider along the bench, giving him full access to her. He wished he could move the table and stand back and see her. He wanted to see how she looked spread eagle on the bench with her pussy peeking from beneath her dress. He was sure the sight of her glistening pussy would be breathtaking.

"They won't know what's going on. Just act like

you're enjoying the music," he chuckled. "That's what you're here for, right? To do some research?"

"Yeah, research for music." She bit back a moan, bringing the back of her hand to her mouth.

"How about we do research to see how fast I can make you come sitting right here." He gently nipped her earlobe. "Let's see how quick you can come and how quiet you can be."

She nodded her head, but he knew that she was totally focused on his hand playing with her pussy.

"I love how wide you have your legs open right now. I can touch every single part of your pussy." He demonstrated by dipping his finger into her channel. He could feel the moisture running down her thighs. He thrust his finger as deep as he could, while using his thumb to continue to strum her clit. "See how wet you are for me? This is all for me. I love how responsive you are to me. Are you imagining my tongue deep within these amazing pussy lips of yours?"

"God, yes." She briefly closed her eyes before opening them again, leaning her head against his shoulder.

"Look out at the crowd. Imagine that they know what's going on beneath the table. Imagine they know that my hand is buried deep in your pussy."

"Sid," she groaned, her chest rising fast. Her hips began to rotate so that she could thrust against his hand.

"Feel how tight you are on my fingers. Imagine me pushing my cock deep inside of you, inch by inch. Your pussy would grip me tight. You want my cock to stretch out this little pussy of yours?"

"Sid," she begged, thrusting her greedy pussy against his hand.

"Ride my hand," he growled. He had meant this to be a quick tease for her, but it had totally backfired on him. He wanted to grab her and slam her down on his cock, but where they were wouldn't allow for that. That would definitely make the news more so than just their difference in race.

"Oh God, I'm about to come," she bit out against her hand. He withdrew his finger from her and concentrated on her clit, moving his fingers across it frantically, applying just enough pressure. Her body stiffened and she closed her eyes as she breathed through her orgasm, without releasing a scream.

"That had to be the most beautiful thing I have ever seen," he murmured in her ear before placing a kiss on her cheek.

She turned her head and met his lips in a hot, searing kiss. He needed to ease up on the passion between them right now. His cock was already thick and heavy, and he was dangerously close to blowing his damn load in his jeans. Her lips parted slightly, but he took advantage of it anyway, pushing his tongue into her mouth. Her tongue met his and coaxed it to duel with hers. His little sex kitten was fucking amazing and blew him away.

He pulled back and gently removed his fingers from her folds, pulling her dress down.

"Sid, you make me do things that I would never have imagined I'd do in a million years." She looked up him. Her face was relaxed, and her demeanor was now laid back.

"I told you that I aim to please you. It gives me pleasure to know that I can take care of you." He kissed her on her forehead, meaning every word he'd said. Bringing her pleasure was enough for him. He knew later, once they got back to the hotel, Nina would be determined to make sure he got his release.

It was that moment when the waiter chose to appear with their food.

Nina's eyes flew to his as she held back a laugh. Had the woman come a minute earlier, she would have been treated to a show. He could see the horror at the realization in Nina's eyes and chuckled. He was sure that the woman had seen much worse in these types of establishments on their busy nights.

The woman made sure that they had everything they needed before disappearing again.

His fingers were still wet from Nina's release, so he licked his fingers clean, loving the taste of her on his tongue.

"Sid." A guttural groan came from Nina as she watched him.

"What? I didn't want to waste that. You're lucky I waited until the waitress was gone," he chuckled as she swatted him with her hand.

"Eat your food," she ordered with a chuckle.

CHAPTER
eighteen

Nina was floating on cloud nine. She couldn't believe that Sid had gotten her off while in the lounge. She could still feel the moisture between her thighs, and her pussy still tingled from her hard release, aching for more. She didn't know how she went through that orgasm without screaming to the high heavens.

Her cheeks hurt so much from smiling and laughing the night away. They were finishing off their second bottle of wine, and Nina would admit to being a little tipsy. The music was catchy. The DJ seemed to know the crowd, and he was amazing working the crowd. She ached to get up and dance, but she didn't want to embarrass Sid by making him uncomfortable by dragging him out onto the dance floor.

She finished off the last of the wine in her glass and placed it on the table. Her body was on autopilot when it came to dancing. She heard a beat and her body would begin to move.

"You having fun?" Sid murmured in her ear. Just the sound of his baritone voice sent shivers down her spine. She couldn't wait for them to get back to the hotel, where she would certainly make him pay. Oh, he would pay dearly.

"I am." She offered her lips to him. When he only gave her a quick kiss, she pouted a little, wanting more, but she would wait.

"Later," he promised, giving into her and laying another one on her lips.

"Look at the lovebirds," a sarcastic voice announced over the music.

Nina froze.

The buzz that she was feeling from the alcohol instantly disappeared. There was no way that she could run into him in Atlanta. She turned her head and there stood Luke. Two men flanked him on each side as he stood there, glaring at Nina and Sid.

Nina could tell that Luke had been drinking, and he was pissed. Luke in a drunken stupor was never good.

"What are you doing here, Luke?" She quickly thought back, and there weren't any major events going on in Atlanta that would require him to be here. Luke owned homes in New York, L.A., and Miami.

"Since you've been avoiding my calls, I figured I would just find out where you were. A little birdie told me you were in Atlanta for a photoshoot. I know you well, Nina. I know how much you love coming here." He gestured around the club. He never liked coming here, but he would to appease her.

"There's nothing for us to talk about," Nina said, shaking her head. She sent up a prayer that he would just leave, but by the looks of it, he wasn't going anywhere without a little force.

"There's plenty to talk about, like why you're still with him." Luke pointed at Sid.

Sid's body stiffened next to her. Her eyes flew around the club, and she found Tank looking her way. She nodded, giving him the green light to get over to them.

"There's no need to signal Tank over here. I just stopped by to speak to my woman," Luke sneered.

"Ex," Sid snapped, his fingers tapping the table slowly. Nina could feel the anger rolling off Sid as he stared into Luke's eyes. Sid was coiled tight, and she knew he was seconds from standing. He hadn't taken too kindly to the last time she'd spoken to Luke on the phone. Sid had been angry that Luke would try to apologize, then insult their relationship by trying to tear it apart.

"What did you say?" Luke snapped, his eyes locked on Sid. Nina could feel Sid moving from behind the table. She tried to hold him back, but there was no way that she would be strong enough.

"No, Sid. He's drunk. He doesn't know what he's saying," she practically yelled. They were officially causing a scene. Most of the patron's eyes were on them. Nina cringed on the inside at the sight of people holding up their phones, recording what was going on. "Luke, go home. You're drunk," she pleaded as Sid stood from the table.

"Naw, let him talk, Nina. I want to hear what he has to say," Luke said, glancing over at her. His eyes were glassed over, and she wasn't sure if he only had alcohol in his system. He turned back to meet Sid. "I'm sorry, what did you say to me, white boy?" Luke growled.

"I said *ex*. She's with me now. How about you leave Nina the hell alone. Stop calling her, and you sure as hell better never come around her again." Sid's voice dropped low as he moved closer to Luke. The two men stood toe to toe, but Sid easily had two to three more inches in height on Luke, and definitely more muscle. The tension surrounding their standoff was palpable.

A sick smile spread across Luke's face that had the bottom of Nina's stomach dropping away.

"How about this. You've had your fun sticking your white dick into my girl. You white boys always want a taste of black pussy, but the games are over. Move the fuck on. Nina's coming with me." Luke, in his drunken stupor, pushed Sid back with both hands. Sid's chest was a solid wall of muscle, and he didn't budge, but she saw the fury in Sid's face as he pulled back his fist.

Nina tried to scramble from the booth as all hell broke loose. She screamed as Sid landed a vicious blow to Luke's face. The two men became a tangle of fists and arms flying through the air. The scuffle grew as the men who were with Luke jumped in.

"Stop!" she screamed, but it was drowned out in the melee. Security converged on the men. Tank plucked her from her seat in the booth, and another guard flanked both sides of her, rushing her through the club as it erupted. She tried to turn to see Sid, but he was lost in the mass of security and observers. "Sid! Stop, Tank! Where's Sid?"

"My men will grab him. You're my priority," Tank growled, pushing her toward the door.

Saying that Sid was pissed was an understatement. He leaned against the ambulance bay, refusing to get in.

"Are you sure you don't want to get checked out at the hospital?" The male EMT asked as he put the last steri-strip on a cut above his eye.

"I'm fine," he growled, scanning the scene for Nina. The scene outside the club was pure chaos. Police lights flashed, highlighting the night sky.

"You're going to be black and blue come morning," the female EMT muttered as she finished cleaning the knuckles on his right hand with antiseptic.

"Won't be the first time," he huffed as he tried to find some sign of Nina. He was sure that the security team got her out to keep her safe.

He hissed at the sting against his knuckles from the medication, but it was well worth it. He would punch Luke Stow in the face again and again if he was given the chance to. Luke and his friends may have tried to beat him down, but they didn't know who they were fucking with. He was able to get in plenty of punches before they converged on him at the same time.

Luke should have fought him one-on-one like a man.

"Sid!" Nina's voice called out. He turned his head, relieved to see her running to him. Her eyes were wide with concern, tears marring her face. He moved away from the EMTs and opened his arms for her. Her body slammed into his.

"Thank God you're okay," she cried out, her face buried into the crook of his neck. He crushed her to his chest. Ignoring the pain, he squeezed her back as her body shook from crying.

"It's okay," he murmured against her head. His eyes caught Tank coming toward them. The fury that lined his face let him know that she must have ran away from her security guard. "I think you're in trouble with Tank."

"I don't care. I was worried about you," she admitted, pulling back from him. She stared up at him as her fingers gently touched his face. He winced slightly as she touched his lips, where he was sure his top lip was a cut. His right eye was heavy, and he knew that soon, it would probably swell shut.

"I can handle myself. I'm just glad that Tank was able to get you out of the way." He ignored the pain in his lip as he laid a gentle kiss on her forehead.

"Well, Tank was trying to do his job, but his employer ducked out on him and ran off," Tank growled, stopping next to them.

"I'm sorry, Tank. I just had to find Sid." She turned her wide eyes to her guard, who melted like butter. Sid knew the feeling. Who could stay mad at Nina?

"Excuse us." Sid turned to the deep voice. Two police officers in their beat uniforms stood next to them. Both men were tall, tanned, and muscular with tattoos visible on their forearms. Nina stiffened in his arms as she looked at who had spoken. "We understand you were involved in the brawl tonight."

"Yeah." Sid kept his voice clipped as he stared at the officers.

"I'm Officer Mahoney and this is Officer Boyd. We'd like to ask you some questions. Please follow us," the other officer said, motioning for them to follow them. Sid nodded and moved behind the officers as they led them to their patrol car.

"I can get my lawyers here within hours if we need them," Nina murmured as she walked next to him. Her grip on his arm was tight as she stayed close to him. Tank followed behind them. Sid was sure Tank was refusing to let Nina out of his sight again.

The arrived at the patrol car, and Officer Mahoney motioned for them to stand by the trunk of the car.

"Can we get your name, sir?" Officer Boyd asked, pulling out his notepad.

"Sidney McFarland," he answered, pulling Nina into his side. She refused to let him go, and at the moment, he felt the same. He needed her next to him so that he could comfort her and calm her fears.

"I understand the fight was between you and a Mr. Luke Stow, is that correct?" Office Mahoney asked, as he too took notes.

"Yes." A few other men that he recognized from Tank's security team kept a distant formation around the cop's car.

The two cops noticed the men too and their eyes narrowed on the men.

"Are they with you?" Officer Boyd asked Sid.

"No, they're with me," Nina chirped. "They're my security team."

"And you are, ma'am?" Officer Mahoney asked, tipping his cap back and studying her closely.

"Nina Hunt," she replied, her lips pressed in a tight line.

"Oh, wow. I'm sorry, ma'am. I didn't recognize you. My wife is a big fan of yours." Officer Boyd finally broke out into a smile as he tipped his hat to Nina.

"Thank you," she remarked. "Are we in trouble?"

"We just need to hear your side of the incident. From what we gathered, Mr. Luke Stow approached your table and confronted you, is that correct?" Officer Mahoney asked. Both of the officers seemed a little bit more relaxed as they probably put two and two together since the brawl involved Luke, and Nina was there.

"Yes. We were enjoying ourselves when he came over to the table and began harassing *my* girlfriend," Sid informed him.

He saw the look that the officers shared at his declaration. He bit back a growl, unsure of the reason behind the look. Was it because she was one of the biggest female singers of all time? Or was it because she was black and he was white? He didn't know why the look, but he knew he didn't like it.

"Please, continue." Officer Boyd motioned as he paused his pen on his pad. Sid narrowed his eyes on him, but a small hand slid across his abdomen, grabbing his attention. He glanced down at Nina who nodded her head for him to continue. She must have known what he was thinking.

"Luke began spouting some insults that were better received if I stood." Sid continued.

"So you felt threatened by Mr. Stow?"

"You're damn straight I did." Sid snorted at the question. Three drunk men standing in front of him and his woman, insulting both him and his woman. That wasn't going to continue. Sid had been waiting for the moment that he would be able to confront Luke.

"Who swung first?" Officer Mahoney asked.

"Luke did," both Sid and Nina answered at the same time.

"Were you there, ma'am?" Officer Boyd asked.

"I told you we were sitting at the table, *together,*" Sid bit out, feeling his anger rising. He clenched his fist at the glance he received from Mahoney.

"There are a ton of witnesses that tell me that Mr. Stow put his hands on you first," Officer Boyd said, flipping back through his notes. Sid began to relax slightly. "Just one last question. Do you want to press charges against Mr. Stow?"

"Yes."

CHAPTER
~nineteen~

Nina sighed as she stepped out of the luxury shower in her hotel suite. Whenever she came to Atlanta, she stayed in the same trendy hotel that offered a presidential suite that allowed her to have complete privacy.

She hadn't gotten much sleep last night since they arrived back from the club. Her phone had been blowing up all night from her family, friends, and her record label. She assured them all that she was unharmed and everything was taken care of. Luke had been arrested on charges of assault, public intoxication, disturbing the peace, along with a few creative charges the police came up with.

Sid had been eerily quiet since they arrived back at the hotel. She wrapped her plush towel around her body before opening the door to the bathroom. They needed to talk.

She stepped into the room and didn't see Sid in the bedroom. He had been asleep when she went into the bathroom. Her heart rate increased as she walked out into the living room and paused without saying a word. Sid, dressed in only his sleeping shorts, was perched on the edge of the couch. She could see faint signs of bruising on his back that she was sure would darken soon. She thought back to the fight, and he'd had the upper hand until Luke's friends jumped in.

Her stomach clenched as she thought of the pain he must be in. All of this was because of her.

She watched as he sat forward on the couch, watching the news with his elbows on his knees. He was so caught up in the news story that he hadn't heard her come into the room.

"Last night, a brawl erupted in the trendy night club, Alter Ego, involving songstress Nina Hunt."

The large flat screen displayed the scene outside the lounge last night, with the flashing lights of police cars and people milling around outside the club.

"Our sources have confirmed that the brawl was between her ex-boyfriend, movie star Luke Stow, and Nina's current boyfriend, Sidney McFarland," the female news anchor announced.

Sources? Who in the hell were their sources?

"This has been festering for a while now. Luke apparently realized the mistake of breaking up with Nina and was trying to get her back. I'm sure it had something to do with that performance of hers at the Writer's Guild ceremony," the male anchor said.

"It must be nice to have two men fight over you. Nina Hunt is one lucky woman," the woman chuckled.

Nina scowled at the woman's comments. Having her man fight her ex was not her idea of fun.

Sid turned the channel and the story of the brawl was on the next station as well. The logo in the corner displayed one of the entertainment channels who had a different version of the news. It was more gossip than anything, and most times, the way they presented the stories were crude and obnoxious. Both of the personalities on the screen were black men discussing what they thought sparked the confrontation.

They jumped to a dark and grainy video from inside the lounge, caught by a bystander, that showed Luke push Sid right before the fight broke out.

"It's one thing for Luke to break up with Nina, but to find out that she's dating a white guy had to be a low blow," the first television personality chuckled.

"Could you imagine that feeling?" The other male laughed. "And then running into her all snuggled up with her personal trainer? Just think, here you are, a huge movie star, and your girl moves on to her personal trainer! I'm not sure which would rub me the wrong way, the fact that she downgraded to a nobody, or that the man hitting that now is white!"

"A woman as fine as Nina Hunt, you know that white boy is tapping that ass." The two men gave each other a high five while they laughed. Nina narrowed her eyes on them, wishing she was a devious woman. How dare they talk about her and Sid in that manner. She rolled her eyes and tried to will her skin to thicken more.

"I'm sure this is just a long publicity stunt. Luke's movie sales have been the lowest they've been in a while," the shorter man said.

"But why would Nina do something like this? She wouldn't have anything to gain from any of this." The other personality shrugged his shoulders.

She held back her curses at the idiots on the television. She didn't need publicity like this.

Sid turned the channel again, this time on another channel who also had the story on. She ought to sick her lawyers on the networks for running such stories that were so racist.

"Sid, turn the TV off." She walked slowly around the couch to him as he flicked it off, throwing the remote across the room. She jumped slightly at the sound of it crashing against the wall.

Tears welled up in her eyes at the sight of him holding his head in his hands. Her heart hurt seeing him like this. All night he tossed and turned in bed. The fight was eating him up, and she wanted to find a way to make him believe that everything was okay. He had defended her against Luke and she wasn't harmed at all.

He didn't say a word as she knelt in front of him. She slowly placed her hands on his wrists to pull his hands away from his head, needing to look into his eyes. Even with the busted lip, swollen black eye and other bruises scattered around his face, she knew she loved him.

A tear slowly fell at the sight of the angered look in his eyes.

"I'm sorry, baby. I didn't mean to cause such a media nightmare for you," he croaked, his face softening as his eyes took her in.

Sliding closer to him, she gripped his head in her hands to force him to look into her eyes. She wanted him to see how much she loved him.

"This is not your fault," she stated, shushing him.

She needed to make him see that his reaction was natural. Luke had said horrible things about them, and Sid was just defending their love. She knew that they would face this kind of behavior from most of society, but the only way they would survive it would be for them to fight for each other, and fight to be together. She didn't give a damn about what the world thought. She loved Sid, and she already knew that he felt the same about her.

"I was just so pissed last night and the alcohol in my system didn't help. I didn't think of the repercussions of my actions. I should have been the better man. I saw that look on Luke's face, heard the words spilling out of his mouth, and all I could think of was smashing my fist in his face to shut him up."

"You were the bigger man. You defended my honor and our relationship. I'm actually glad you punched him in his face. It's been long overdue." She smiled softly, brushing the lone tear from her face. His face relaxed at her comment. "Don't worry about the media. If he would've just talked to me and left, the media would be blowing that all out of proportion as well, coming up with a crazy tale. That's just what they do. This will blow over. I spoke to my lawyer a couple of hours ago, and they'll handle any of the potential lawsuits. I don't anticipate any. I've already offered to pay for all damages that occurred at the club."

Sid blew out a deep breath and sat back against the couch. She stood from the floor and crawled onto the couch, tossing her leg over his to straddle his waist.

"All night. I kept thinking that I should've just grabbed your hand and taken you out of the club. But those things he kept saying—"

"Was to provoke you, make him feel like the bigger man. Luke can't handle being outdone," she murmured, putting her finger to his lips to silence him. She could see the anger mounting in his eyes. He must have been replaying Luke's words in his head.

She'd had to hold back her laughter last night when she watched the police handcuff and put Luke in the back of the patrol car. He fought them the whole way, spewing that he would sue the city of Atlanta.

"He realized that he made a mistake. I'm sure he thought that I would pine after him forever," she said.

"Well, he's going to have to live with his mistake forever. He was stupid to give you up, but I will never be that stupid, Nina. You're my woman. No matter what they say about us, I love you and want you in my life forever."

"You love me?" she asked quietly. She had already known by his actions that he did, but to hear him finally say the words made her heart sing.

He gathered her to him, bringing her head down to his. His blue eyes searched hers as he tucked a strand of her hair behind her ear.

"I have loved you since our first date," he murmured, then chuckled. "This wasn't how I imagined me confessing my love to you."

She burst out laughing. "You were going to confess your love to me?"

"It's not funny. I'm trying to be serious." He tenderly cupped her cheek in his hand as he stared into her eyes.

She could feel herself grow slick with need for him. It didn't matter that this man had went to war for her last night, and was now battered and bruised.

She loved him.

"I love you too, Sid." His face relaxed at her admission. "I've known for a while that you loved me. I didn't need the words, but it's good to finally hear them out loud." She gently brushed her fingertips along his eye that was swollen shut, down to the bruising that surround it, then down to the cut and swollen top lip.

She felt him harden beneath her and her eyes flew to his. The only barrier between them was was his shorts.

"Nina," he murmured, reaching up to untuck the towel. It fell away, leaving her naked on his lap. "I need you."

Those three words ripped her heart wide open. The stark need in his eyes told her that this was more than just sex. It was a connection on a level only the two of them could reach.

Together.

She needed him too. She had been used to the world picking her life apart just because she was in the public eye. But to pick apart her relationship with the man she loved just because of their skin color, it rubbed her raw and left her feeling vulnerable.

She leaned forward and placed a soft kiss on his lips as he filled his hands with the swell of her ass. He murmured her name again as she moved her hips, guiding her heat along the hard length of him.

"I don't want to hurt your lip." Placing another soft

kiss on his mouth, he reached up with one hand and cupped her breast in his hand, bringing it to his mouth. He trailed his tongue around her dark areola before nipping her taut nipple with his teeth. She threw back her head and moaned as she felt the moisture seep out of her core. He worshiped her breast while guiding her along his length. The fabric from his shorts created a sweet friction between her legs.

"Sid," she gasped, needing more. She wanted to feel him deep within her, and didn't want to be teased any longer.

"Take what you need, baby," he growled against her flesh.

She reached down and pulled at the drawstring of his shorts. It finally gave way and fell apart. She reached inside his shorts and pulled his beautiful stiff cock out. It was absolutely gorgeous, and long enough to hit the deepest part of her pussy, satisfying her like no man had ever done before.

She positioned herself over him and slowly impaled herself onto him. They both groaned once she became seated fully.

"I love you," he gasped, gripping her tight in his hands.

"I love you too," she murmured as he guided her along his cock.

He allowed her to set the rhythm of their lovemaking. She didn't want fast. They had all day, and she wanted to take her time with him. She wanted to make sure that he knew just how much she loved him. She leaned forward, grabbing the back of the couch to help give her leverage as she slid up and down on his length. Her pussy burned slightly from being stretched to the brim, but it wasn't a painful burn. It was one that she was addicted to. It let her know that she was made to take him, by the way he fit so snug inside of her.

"Take it all," he growled against her chest as she began to pick up the pace.

He thrust up, pushing his cock deeper. Her breaths came fast as he began to pound into her. She realized that she was no longer in control. She could see from his expression that he needed to take her. She wanted him to know that she belonged to him and that he could do what he wanted with her. Right now, the look in his eye suggested that he wanted to possess her.

"Yes, Sid!"

She wanted him to mark her, make her his in every way. He slammed her down hard on his cock, the speed increasing. Her grip on the couch tightened as she took everything he gave her. His thrusts became hard, almost desperate. She could feel her muscles grow tight as a euphoric feeling washed over her.

"Please, make me come," she chanted. She was so

close. His hand slid between them, and she felt his finger part her folds to play with her swollen clit.

"Let go, Nina. Go ahead a fall apart in my arms. I'll catch you," he growled. She screamed as the sensations became too much for her. Her body trembled as she rode out the waves of her orgasm. He shouted as he joined her, pouring his warm release into her. Her body collapsed on his as he held her tight to him.

They lay still, no words were needed as time passed. The silence was beautiful to Nina. They had finally confessed their love to each other. She couldn't see herself with no other man but Sid. His large hand stroked her back, sending chills down her spine. His semihard cock was still buried inside of her and she didn't want to move. They completed each other, and the feel of them still joined made her feel whole.

"Don't let me go," she murmured against his neck.

"Never, baby. Never."

CHAPTER
twenty

Camera flashes blinded Nina as she stepped out of the limousine. The media clamored for her attention as she walked the carpet.

Her album, *Nina,* was officially available for purchase. This was one of her most personal albums to date, and she couldn't be prouder of herself.

"This is a madhouse," Sid murmured in her ear as they paused in front of the wall that housed the name of her sponsors for her album release party.

"I guess I can officially welcome you to my world." She smiled as he pulled her close under the crook of his arm. She had a hard time staying away from him, and he cleaned up pretty good.

His tailored black suit fit him perfectly. He topped off the suit with a black, button-down shirt, with the first two buttons undone. It drove her wild.

"I think I like the shadows much better," he chuckled, laying a kiss on the top of her head. "How long do we have to be here? This dress of yours is causing my pants to get a little tight."

She batted him away as she headed toward the throng of fans that lined the security gates, making sure to add a little more sass in her walk. She knew that he loved her dress the minute she had stepped out of the bedroom of their hotel suite.

Her see-through, black mini dress, molded to her body, showing off her curves that Sid had helped her achieve. Black thigh-high boots complimented her outfit.

She was fierce.

She blew Sid a kiss and turned to her fans. They screamed and cried out as she began signing autographs and snapping selfies with her adoring fans.

"It's time to go in," Tank announced, coming to her side. She blew kisses at her fans as she followed her bodyguard into the night club.

Nina gasped as she entered the establishment. Tasha spared no expense on this place. The air in the club was electric, and all of the top industry people were present. She walked through, recognizing familiar faces of other celebrities in the industry.

She knew Sid didn't like being in the limelight, so she made sure he found a safe, quiet corner to relax in and enjoy the party.

"Nina! The album is on fire!" A voice came up behind her.

"Scott!" she cried out, going straight into his open arms. She squeezed him tight as he hugged her. "I'm so glad you made it."

"I wouldn't miss this for anything in world." He laughed. "Good job."

"Thanks for coming to my rescue and helping me with it," she said, genuinely thankful for him and all the people that helped her with this project. "It means a lot."

"Now don't go all sentimental on me. All I ask is that you return the favor when I jump back into the studio." He hugged her one last time before Tank began leading her through the crowd.

It never failed to amaze her to hear her vocals on the soundwaves. After all the years of being in the business, she should have been used to it.

Tank led her to the upper lounge that was reserved for her and her closest friends and family. Her eyes met Sid's as he leaned against the balcony that looked down to the main floor of the club. She could feel the heat from his gaze as she made her way to him.

"You're an amazing woman," he murmured, pulling her to him. She smiled as he leaned down and placed a gentle kiss on her lips. The bruises he had received in Atlanta had healed, leaving a small scar right about his lip. She made sure to kiss it as often as possible to apologize for him getting hurt.

"I already warned you before," she whispered against

his lips. "If you mess up my makeup, Sebastian might claw your eyes out." The sides of Sid's eyes crinkled as he barked out a laugh. Her makeup artist did not play when it came to ruined makeup.

"Baby, I think—no, I know I can take Sebastian," he advised as she turned her back to him. She wanted to get a glimpse of everyone who came out to support her album release. The party was in full swing, with people dancing on the dance floor. The bar was packed and everyone was having a great time.

"Nina!" She turned to see Meg barreling toward her.

"What's up, Meg?" Nina asked, leaning back against Sid. She knew it was a mistake when she felt his steel rod brushing against the swell of her ass.

"You broke the internet!" Meg exclaimed.

"What?" she shrieked, taking Meg's tablet from her. Online news reports were claiming that because of her sudden release, servers from the major online retailers were not equipped to handle the influx of traffic to their sites, therefore causing them to crash.

She jumped in place, screaming with her sister to celebrate the album's success.

"This is crazy." Meg laughed. "My sister actually broke the internet."

"Did you hear this?" She turned to Sid with a wide grin. He leaned over her shoulder to read the stories on the internet with her.

"Baby, this is fucking amazing." His warm breath tickled the back of her neck as she scrolled the screen.

Her finger paused at a story that discussed Luke and his continuing legal troubles. His charges for assaulting Sid at the Atlanta club a couple months ago were just the beginning. The IRS had recently brought up charges against him for tax evasion. The article talked about one of his homes being liquidated to pay back owed taxes.

It all made sense, why all of a sudden he'd called her to get back with her.

He didn't love her.

She had been a financial ticket for him. He would have tried to get back in her good graces, and had it not been for Sid, she probably would have fallen for it. They had been together for so long, she would have tried to make their failed relationship work.

She stared down at the picture of her ex and shook her head. She'd thought she was in love with him, but now that she looked back, she knew it wasn't love.

"You all right?" Sid asked, bringing her closer to him as she read the story.

"Yes, I'm good." She smiled, getting down to the end of the story.

"Finally! Celebratory champagne," Meg yelled as a waitress walked up to them with flutes filled with champagne.

Nina grabbed her flute, an excited grin plastered

across her face as she looked at her family and friends surrounding her.

"Hey, Nina!" a familiar voice called out over the microphone.

She glanced down over the railing and saw Vin standing up on the stage, waving to her. She laughed as she waved back at him.

"Attention everyone!" Vin called out again, getting the attention of the patrons in the club. The talking died down and the music was lowered. "Good evening, everyone. I just want to take a few minutes to give a toast to the woman of the night, Nina Hunt."

The club broke out into excited chatter and clapping as everyone glanced up at the balcony at her. She smiled and waved down to everyone. Sid's arm around her hugged her side as she leaned into him.

"Nina, you are amazing to work with. You were focused, you knew what you wanted, and it made my job easier. This is one hell of an album, and by the sounds of the news, you just broke the internet tonight! Who in the hell does that? Apparently, our girl Nina does!"

Laughter and cheers filled the air at the mention of the platforms crashing from the rush of people trying to download her latest album.

"Nina, please do us the honor and get down here and sing us a song off this latest album!"

The crowd began to chant her name. She smiled,

loving the electric atmosphere of the club. She glanced up at Sid and smiled. She loved him so much.

"Looks like they're calling me." She laughed.

"Go knock them dead, baby," he murmured, laying a kiss on her forehead.

"Oh, I will," she giggled as she rushed off.

Sid sipped his drink as he watched Nina meet her producer Vin on the stage. The crowd was antsy as they waited for her to begin her song. Nina was all smiles as she stepped up to the mike. Her band filed onto the stage, each getting ready to perform.

"I just want to thank everyone for coming out tonight," she said to the crowd. Cheers filled the air in response to her words. "I know you've heard so many things in the media for a while now about me and my life. I just want to let everyone know I'm good right now."

The crowd cheered and clapped, hollering out their love for Nina.

The band began to play a slow song. She swayed to the music, her eyes meeting his. He tilted his glass to her as she closed her eyes and opened her mouth to allow her song to come forth. It was his favorite song on her album, and he knew that she had been thinking of them when she wrote it.

As she sang and began working the crowd, he moved from where he was perched. He made his way down the crowded stairwell toward the main floor of the club.

When I'm on the road, I miss you.
You're never far from my mind.
Your baby blues makes me shiver.
The thought of your touch makes me tingle.
I need you.
Deep inside of me.
I need you.
Gotta find my way back to you.

Her voice captivated everyone in the club. He kept his eyes on her as he made his way to the stage and stood off to the side where she couldn't see him. He had been trying to decide when would be the best time to do what he had planned, and felt that this was the perfect moment.

This is our love story.
I'll always come back to you.
This is our love story.
I'll always rush to be with you.
This is our love story.
I'll always love you.

Sid walked out onto the stage from the side where she couldn't see him. He smiled to members of her band who returned the gesture. The excitement in the air grew as the crowd saw him, and most must have recognized him from all the exposure in the media. He reached in his pocket and brought out something that he'd had for weeks now. He unfastened his jacket button and got down on one knee and waited.

Now the crowd was causing such a ruckus that Nina turned to see what the fans were pointing at.

She froze in place at the sight of him.

The mic fell from her hands as her eyes met his.

He held up the ring in his hand as she slowly walked toward him.

"Is that a..." She gulped, unable to finish her words as she came to a halt in front of him.

He had thought long and hard about how he would finally get up the courage to make their relationship official.

"Nina Ann Hunt." His heart pounded in his chest as he realized that almost every person in the club had their phone out and was recording them.

"Sid," she murmured, her hands flying to her face. Her eyes glistened as they filled with trapped tears that had yet to fall.

"I love you more than life itself. You've brightened up my life and made me realize that I cannot live without you. Please, would you do me the honor of becoming my wife?" he asked.

She flew into his arms as a cry broke from her lips. He gathered her to him as he stood, her body trembling as he pulled back to hear her answer.

"Yes! Yes! Yes!" she shouted as she jumped in place. He laughed as she held her hand out for him to slip the ring onto her finger.

The crowd went wild, hearing that she had accepted his proposal. She jumped into his arms and wrapped hers tight around his neck.

"Don't let me go," she murmured against his ear.

"Never, baby. Never,"

The End.

LETTER TO THE READER

Thank you for taking the time to read Pieces Of Me. I hope you enjoyed Nina and Sid's story! I hope that you will also take a few minutes and leave a review for this book.

I love reading reviews so what readers think of the books they read! Every review matters!

If you would like to stay up to date with me and my work, check out my Facebook page www.facebook.com/peytonbanksauthor.

Again, thank for reading Pieces of Me!

Warm wishes,
Peyton Banks

SNEAK PEEK

Summer Escape
by Peyton Banks

Marina Carter gazed upon the clear blue ocean on display before her. It was a perfect way to spend her morning. Stretched out on the white sandy beach with her toes buried deep in the sand was how she wished she could spend all of her days. But she knew reality waited for her at home.

She was a coward. A chicken.

She glanced down at her naked ring finger on her left hand and let out a long, deep sigh. The ring was gone. She didn't know how she truly felt about it, but she was glad that it hadn't went further than an engagement.

Three days ago, she had walked into her fiancé's apartment and found him on the couch with his pants around his ankles, and a blonde swallowing his cock.

She had always known that their relationship was

one of convenience, and that night was just what she needed to move on. She knew of the countless women that he tried to hide from her, and she had always turned a blind eye to it. They hadn't even been intimate with each other in months. But this was a firm reason to end what they had between them.

Her father, Thomas Carter, was a prominent senator in Washington. Her fiancé, Vincent Snider, was a wealthy business tycoon. Between the two of them, Marina had let them talk her into an engagement. She and Vin had dated off and on for years throughout college, but it was at the urging of her father that she really considered a life with Vin. They thought it would be the perfect merger of a business tycoon and a senator's daughter.

Not anymore.

She'd had every intention of breaking up with him when she went over to his condo. She knew that he would have argued with her, and blamed it on her emotions. Her father would have called and insisted they needed to work out their problems, citing that every couple had doubts before their wedding.

She snorted as she reached for her mimosa, and took a healthy sip.

She had been engaged for a full year, and had yet to even begin planning a wedding. What woman gets engaged and doesn't get excited about planning her wedding?

It was time she took back her life. She loved her father dearly, and she knew he had done the best he could since her mother passed when she was a teenager.

But no more.

The muffled ringing of her phone grabbed her attention. She reached over and rifled through her bag as the ringing got louder.

Favorite Bitch was displayed across the screen. A wide grin spread across her face. "Marina's private line, how can I help you?" she answered with a smile. She leaned back against the lounge chair and took another sip of her refreshing drink.

"Have you lost your mind?" Claire Legarde demanded.

"Why no, I have not, Claire Bear," she chuckled, using her best friend's nickname.

Claire and Marina had met during their freshman year in college, and had become lifelong friends. She knew that she could count on Claire to have her back.

"That asshat of yours has been blowing up my phone looking for you. Where the hell are you? I went by your place. Your bedroom looks like it was ransacked, and I haven't see you in two days! Are you okay?" Claire practically screamed in her ear.

She did feel a little guilty for just leaving the way she

did. She had rushed home that night after watching the blonde release Vin's cock from her mouth as he scrambled off his couch.

"It's over. I'm done." She had uttered four little words, but they had held such a punch. She turned on her heels and marched out of the condo to the sounds of Vin yelling her name.

"I'm fine, Claire. I promise. It's over between me and that asshat. This was long overdue, and going over to his place the other night and finding some bitch sucking him off was all I needed to finally put an end to that dreaded relationship," she said, placing her now empty glass down on the table beside her.

"Oh, shit," Claire breathed.

"Don't worry, I'll be fine." And she would be. She was at a private resort with lots of people she could meet and mingle with. Nothing like good fresh air to help wake up all the common sense a girl was born with.

"But where the hell are you?" Claire's voice broke through her thoughts. Marina looked around at the beach that was lined with early risers, relaxing in the sun.

"Well, about that. I just happen to be in the Bahamas," she admitted, pulling the phone away from her ear as her friend let out a loud shriek.

"Are you fucking kidding me? You took the time to pack a suitcase, made arrangements for flight and hotel, and not once did you think to pick up the phone and invite me along?"

"I needed this, some alone time to clear my mind and thoughts. I need to figure out what the hell I'm doing." She closed her eyes as she leaned her head back against her lounge chair.

Yeah, that was what she needed, to clear her mind and just breathe. Get away from the harsh realities of the life she had left back in Baltimore, and figure out what she should do next.

"Still, it's not fair. You're living the life in one of the most beautiful places on Earth, and I'm stuck here. I have half a mind to hop a plane and join you. The island is big enough for both of us. I'd stay on my side, you'd stay on yours."

Marina chuckled at her friends' dramatics.

"You could if you want, but all the sexy men would gravitate to me," she teased, tossing her brunette hair over her bare shoulder.

"Bitch," Claire retorted.

"I'm your favorite bitch," she replied with a laugh.

"You got that fucking right. So, what do you have planned, Stella? Getting your groove back?"

"I don't know. I've been loyal to Vin for the past few years. I wouldn't even know how to date." She blew out a breath. Did she need to jump back into a relationship?

She could just date and get to know people with no strings attached.

"Let me give you a hint of what to do. Find a hot guy. Walk up to hot guy. Introduce yourself to hot guy, then ask if you can hop on his dick."

Marina burst out laughing, tears streaming down her face. Damn, she should have told Claire about the trip. They would have had a blast together.

"Okay, I'll remember that," she said, finally able to speak. She wiped her tears away from her face. Her phone beeped, signaling another call. She quickly glanced at the screen and her laughter instantly faded.

Dad.

"Hey, Claire Bear, I gotta go. My father is on the other line." She knew what was coming. She was sure Vin had run to her father with the news. Thomas Carter may be a big-time senator in Washington, but this one time, she wouldn't let him make a decision for her. Her life was hers, and it was time she took control of it.

"Okay. Call me whenever, just so I know your safe."

"Will do."

ABOUT THE AUTHOR

Peyton Banks is the alter ego of a city girl who is a romantic at heart.

Her mornings consist of coffee and daydreaming up the next steamy romance book ideas.

She loves spinning romantic tales of hot alpha males and the women they love.

Make sure you check her out!

Want to know the latest about Peyton Banks?

Follow her on Facebook:

ALSO BY PEYTON BANKS

Stand Alone Books

Summer Escape

Pieces of Me

Hard Love (Coming 2018)

A Tokhan Bratva Series

Unexpected Allies (Coming 2018)

Unexpected Chaos (Coming 2018)

Unexpected Hero (TBD)

Special Weapons & Tactics Series

Dirty Tactics (2018)

Dirty Ballistics (TBD)